Praise for Harriso

"There's a lot to like in Joseph L.S. Terrell's *Calling Cards Of Death*: Mystery, romance, intrigue, history, snappy dialogue, and even a heartfelt love letter to Paris and North Carolina's Outer Banks. A great beach read, in more ways than one!"
—Richard Helms, Derringer and Thriller Award-Winning Author of *Brittle Karma*

Undertow of Vengeance, Joseph Terrell's fourth thriller in the Harrison Weaver crime writer series, and set in North Carolina's Outer Banks, is a knockout. With the deadpan savvy delivery of Humphrey Bogart as Sam Spade and the clipped declarative sentences of Dashiell Hammett, this volume, like its predecessors, reaches out in the very first sentence, grabs you by the lapels, and never lets up.
—Joseph Bathanti, former North Carolina Poet Laureate

Smooth writing from an eloquent storyteller goes down like fine scotch. *Undertow of Vengeance* is a keeper.
—Maggie Toussaint, Author, Cleopatra Jones Mysteries

"Every once in a while I'll pick up a book and from the first sentence, I'm engaged. Written with an extraordinary eye for detail yet in the sparse language of the journalist he once was, Terrell's novel is filled with wonderful dialogue, believable characters and just enough plot twists to keep the reader turning pages."
—Kip Tabb, Freelance Writer, former Ed. *North Beach Sun*

"Joe Terrell gets the Outer Banks just right, from crashing surf to the sordid crimes behind the tourism façade, to a thoughtful sleuth who can throw a punch and make a mean sweet tea."
—David Healey, Author, *The House That Went Down With The Ship*

"A smart, savvy combination of who-done-it and police procedural."
—Kathryn R. Wall, Author, the Bay Tanner Mysteries

Books by
Joseph L.S. Terrell

Harrison Weaver Mysteries

TIDE OF DARKNESS
OVERWASH OF EVIL
NOT OUR KIND OF KILLING
UNDERTOW OF VENGEANCE
DEAD RIGHT RETURNING
THE LAST BLUE NOON IN MAY
DEADLY DREAMS OF SUMMER
CALLING CARDS OF DEATH
THE SOUVENIR KEEPER

Mary Ann Little Weaver Mysteries

THE SERPENTINE FLOWER
A FLOWER SO FALLEN

Jonathan Clayton Novels

THE OTHER SIDE OF SILENCE
LEARNING TO SLOW DANCE

Stand Alones

A TIME OF MUSIC, A TIME OF MAGIC

A NEUROTIC'S GUIDE TO SANE LIVING

The Souvenir Keeper

A HARRISON WEAVER MYSTERY

JOSEPH L.S. TERRELL

BellaRosaBooks

THE SOUVENIR KEEPER
ISBN 978-1-62268-167-9

First Printed: June 2021

Also available as e-book: ISBN 978-1-62268-168-6

Cover illustration by Roo Harris.
Author photograph by Lynne Scott Constantine.

Book design by Bella Rosa Books.

10   9   8   7   6   5   4   3   2   1

This book is for Gail Hutchison, Victim's Advocate for Dare County Sheriff's Office, and for the others who voluntarily devote support to victims of assault.

Author's Note:

This is a work of fiction, and although I have used the names of a few real people, the main characters, while very much alive to me, are purely the product of my imagination. Most of the places I mention are real, but as I have done in the past, I have compressed time to depict the historic Dare County Courthouse as it used to be used—to house the sheriff's office as well as other county departments.

–*JLST*

Acknowledgement:

I would like to extend a special thanks to Gail Hutchison, Victim's Advocate for the Dare County Sheriff's Office, for helping me with many of the details of her work with sexual assault victims, and to first manuscript readers Cathy Kelly and Veronica Moschetti Reich for their insight and catches with the first draft of this work; their keen eyes help. Also, thanks to former FBI agent Larry Likar for supplying research material concerning serial rapists, and to professional videographer and drone operator Benny Baldwin, who can make those devices come alive. An acknowledgment would be far from complete without the deepest thanks to professional concept editor and talented author Jaden (Beth) Terrell for her tireless work in making this a better story. She is the best. And once again, my sincerest appreciation to Rod Hunter, publisher of Bella Rosa Books, for his continuing support and faith in me as a writer.

–*JLST*

The
Souvenir
Keeper

Chapter One

"There's been another one," Chief Deputy Odell Wright said. He sagged with the weight of what had obviously been an all-night investigation. Flecks of silver whiskers caught the sunlight that touched his coffee-colored skin. Sweat stains rimmed the collar of his uniform shirt. His eyelids looked heavy, as if crusted with sand.

We stood outside the Budleigh Street side entrance to the Dare County Courthouse. It was before nine o'clock on a Wednesday morning.

There was only one case in the past few months shocking enough for him to expect me to know what he meant by *another one*. I stood close. "Raped? Murdered?"

He nodded.

"Who?"

"Trigger Massey."

I stiffened as if smacked. "What? Jeeze . . . You got to be . . ." My voice raised. "I know her . . . knew her."

"Lot a people did," he said.

He spoke so softly I could hardly hear him, and there was something like a humming in my ears. Overriding the sadness I felt about Trigger's fate was a deep and growing anger. Not a flash of anger, but a smoldering, steadily intensifying rage. My fists were clenched so tight my fingernails dug into the palms of my hands. The anger was directed at the son of a bitch who had done this—violated her body and snuffed out her life.

Trigger Massey—I don't know what her actual first name was, just the nickname "Trigger"—had worked as a waitress or hostess at several of the restaurants. She was so personable and friendly she impressed everyone who met her. She wore her light brown hair almost shoulder length. Her hair was full and rich, and at probably thirty years of age, was threaded with a few gray hairs. But she grinned that she'd earned them.

Odell put a hand on the doorknob. "I've got to see the sheriff," he said.

"Let me come up with you." We entered and started up the back stairs. "I had an appointment with the sheriff to talk about an article, but I'm sure he'll want to cancel. Got to."

"I expect so," Odell said. He trudged up the stairs. I knew he had to be worn out, but he appeared determined to hold his shoulders back and stand erect. A tough guy and a hell of a good lawman.

The article I wanted to talk with Sheriff Eugene Albright about could certainly wait. This latest killing occupied front and center.

My name is Harrison Weaver and I'm a crime writer. I make my home now on North Carolina's Outer Banks, a one-hundred-mile strip of narrow barrier islands that stretch north to south between the ocean and the Albemarle and Pamlico sounds.

At the top of the stairs, Mabel met us. She stood in the hall outside the sheriff's office. The tiniest shake of her head said it all, and mirrored my thoughts as well. *The world's going to hell in a hand basket.*

Mabel has been with the sheriff's department for a hundred years or more. She knows more about what's going on than anyone else. As usual, she wore a loose-fitting pullover top and those soft-soled comfortable black shoes that ran over on the sides. The shoes favored her ankles, which were perpetually swollen. In the past year or so she announced she was through with dieting for the rest of her life.

"He's expecting you," she said to Odell.

We both stepped inside the sheriff's office and stood in front of his desk. Sheriff Eugene Albright didn't bother getting up. He nodded toward the two chairs in front of his desk. Albright is a big bear of a man with a large, broad face. His bulk and size are intimidating until you see, and sense, the kindness behind his eyes. I've said before he'd much rather counsel young offenders than arrest them.

He appeared ready to address Odell but then paused midway before speaking and turned to me. "I know we had an appointment but—"

"Yes, sir," I said. "I understand."

He didn't indicate any objection, or even surprise, I was there in the room. Albright and others are so used to seeing me around the courthouse they pay little attention to my presence.

"Okay, tell me." Albright directed his gaze at his deputy. Before Odell could start to give a rundown, the sheriff effectively stopped him by raising the palm of one hand. "Next of kin?"

"No one close," Odell said. "Parents deceased. No siblings. A cousin out in New Mexico or some place."

Sheriff Albright's face registered relief. Freed from the emotional heart-rending notification of next of kin.

Odell watched the sheriff a moment, then proceeded. "Preliminary, but I think it's the same guy—the one who did the Ferguson woman."

He referred to the rape and murder two months earlier of Francine Ferguson, a single woman also of about thirty, whose body was discovered in her burning house. At first, it was assumed she might have died from smoke inhalation. But the fire was confined mostly in the living room and front hall and there was not much smoke. Autopsy results showed there was no smoke in her lungs, and her throat had bruises. Facial distortions also indicated she had been strangled, as the autopsy confirmed. Odell had never closed the investigation into this unsolved killing. The case became dominant in Odell's thinking; it took front and center with him, and I knew that.

Sheriff Albright said, "A fire? There wasn't any fire this time, was there?"

"No, there wasn't." Odell gave a tiny shake of his head, almost more of a shrug. "Not that he didn't try. No accelerant. Instead, the guy tried using the old cigarette and paper matches incendiary."

A puzzled Albright.

Odell said, "You light a cigarette, wedge the mouth-end under the head of the matches. When the cigarette burns all the way up, it ignites the matches with a big flame and starts a fire." He gave a mirthless chuckle. "This guy used one of Trigger's cigarettes and put the . . . the device near some wadded-up papers—but the cigarette went out before it reached the matches."

"So much for that," Albright said.

"I got a feeling he won't even try to start a fire next time."

"There can't ever be 'next time,'" Albright said. "We can't have any more of this."

Odell said, "I know, I know. But he's getting bolder. From everything I've read and heard about serial killers, they don't slow down once they get started. They keep it up. Get to thinking they're smarter than police. I figure he'll try again . . ." Weariness dragged down his voice.

A gentle tap, and Mabel pushed open the door a few inches. "Agent Twiddy returned your call, Sheriff. He's on his way here."

"Good," Albright said.

He turned to Odell and started to speak, but Odell beat him to it. "We can sure use him."

Albright nodded, more relaxed.

They referred to State Bureau of Investigation Agent T. (for Thomas) Ballsford Twiddy. His friends call him Balls, which they feel is a more descriptive moniker for him than simply the shortening of Ballsford. He's a big, tough guy and has earned the respect of plenty of other cops. He and I have been good friends for years, ever since my newspaper reporting days. His outward gruffness is almost a cliché in that it does indeed mask a warmness of heart that lies underneath. I had been fortunate enough and lucky enough to furnish information to him that helped in his solving an extremely puzzling case. Since then, he has permitted me to hang with him on a number of investigations, knowing I won't write anything before it is time. I know when to keep my mouth shut, and when to keep the cap on my pen.

Odell continued briefing the sheriff. "The body's on the way to Greenville for an autopsy. Dr. Willis was there about two this morning. Hated to call him." Odell gave a shake of his head. "Old Doc Willis still manages to respond to these middle of the night calls."

Sheriff Albright said, "He's getting pretty old to be doing this coroner stuff."

"Anyway, he's sure she was raped—or at least had had sex." Odell cleared his throat. "No visible trace of semen. Autopsy'll determine some details on that." He cleared his throat again. "Also, Dr. Willis thinks she was manually strangled. Bruises on the neck, and you know, the way her eyes bulged, flecks of blood."

Odell paused and looked down at his folded hands, as if remembering details of the room, the body. I imagined it also, something I do vividly when someone is describing a scene. I can picture it. Useful as a writer; sometimes painful as a caring human being. Mentally picturing Trigger dead did not come easy. I could still see her smiling and greeting men and women alike as "sweetie" or "honey." That smoldering anger rose again over her violated life.

Odell glanced up at the sheriff, but really appeared to be staring off in the distance above and beyond the sheriff. "Positioning of the body, placing the arms out to the sides— like the earlier one, the Ferguson woman."

"Photographs?" Albright said.

"Oh, yes sir. Deputy Dorsey must have taken a thousand . . . with our new digital camera. They'll be on my computer. And I'll print out a few hard copies."

Sheriff Albright waited a moment. "The boyfriend?"

Odell shook his head. "We'll talk with her boyfriend—and former boyfriends. But if it is what I think it is—the same perpetrator—then that eliminates the boyfriend, in my mind."

Albright shook his head, as if he could ward something off. "Let's don't even mention serial killer, or serial rapist."

Odell took a breath. "Just the same—"

With the palms of both hands, Albright motioned downward toward the top of his desk, as if pressing away the thought of a serial killer. "Don't even . . ."

Mabel stepped up to the doorway again. "Sorry to interrupt, Sheriff, but we're already getting press calls—*The Virginian-Pilot*, Jeff with *The Daily Advance*. Mary Ann Little up in Currituck. And some TV guy."

Sheriff Albright shook his head. "Doesn't take 'em long, does it?"

Mabel continued standing there in the doorway, waiting.

Albright looked at Odell. "Press conference? This afternoon? We can't tell 'em anything . . . anything other than confirm a slaying, investigation ongoing."

"Almost gotta," Odell said. "One o'clock? Agent Twiddy will be here also."

"Okay," Albright said. He turned his face toward Mabel. "Handle it, please."

"Certainly," she said, and shuffled away toward her tiny office.

The sheriff and Odell were winding up their conversation. I stood when Odell did. He told the sheriff he would certainly keep him informed, and would see him again when Agent Twiddy arrived and before the press conference.

As Odell and I stepped toward the door, former district

attorney Rick Schweikert appeared.

He glared hard at me before turning that lip-raised smile of his toward the sheriff.

No love lost between Schweikert and me. Not a bit.

Chapter Two

The animosity between Schweikert and me dated back about four years, when I first moved to the Outer Banks. I had profiled him—quite accurately—in an article as a pompous, holier-than-thou, neo-fascist. He had it in for me ever since. Once even tried to implicate me in the killing of a local radio personality.

As Odell and I went into his office, he muttered under his breath, "Saw the look your buddy Schweikert gave you." He permitted himself the briefest of a wry grin.

Atop his gunmetal gray desk, I saw the Francine Ferguson file. He followed my gaze. He hadn't sat down. "Still going over that last night when the call came through about the Massey woman."

I hesitated, then said, "I'd like to go over that file, too, if you don't mind."

He shrugged. "Might be helpful. Fresh eyes, you know." Then he seemed to weigh that thought. "Best not to make a big deal out of looking at it though. Don't think there's anything, you know, confidential in there that you don't already know, but just the same . . ."

"Discreet," I said. "I'll be discreet."

"You can use the next office," he said, indicating with the slant of a thumb toward the small room used mostly for interrogations. Three metal chairs and one metal table. No windows.

"Be fine," I said, and took the file folder he handed over to me. The file was about two inches thick. Two or three loose pages bulged out at the bottom of the folder. They were rather dog-eared.

"Photos," Odell said, and handed me a separate brown envelope, hefty with printouts of what I assumed were scene shots. "Of course, they moved the body real quick because of the fire, and they didn't know for sure she was dead. But not that much smoke, and the fire was up toward the front of the house. One of the volunteers used his phone to shoot a couple of pictures overall. Not the greatest, but you can see some of the scene before it was completely compromised."

I started to the door.

Odell still hadn't sat down. It was as if he thought he might not be able to rise again if he sat. He said, "I'll check with the sheriff, and then head home to take a shower, change clothes, and return before the press conference." He paused, one hand in his pocket rattling coins or keys, thinking. "Agent Twiddy'll be here probably before I get back." He stopped rattling the coins. "You can keep him entertained meantime." He glanced about to make sure he wasn't forgetting something. Then both of us left his office. He went toward the sheriff's office and I went left to the interrogation room, two folders tucked under my arm.

I plopped down in one of the two chairs facing the table, spreading the two folders in front of me. I didn't open either one of them. What I really wanted to do was go downstairs to the Register of Deeds office and see my sweetheart Elly. That's Ellen ("Elly") Pedersen, and I guess now that I've finally given her that ring I carried around for weeks—more than a month—before finding what I thought was the special occasion to give it to her, that she's more than a sweetheart. Heck, fiancée? Well, tell the truth we haven't really decided yet. Anyway, I'd see her before the press conference, I was sure.

I sighed and opened the file folder with the notes, reports of interviews, newspaper clippings, autopsy report and other odds and ends. I had seen some of this material before. Carefully, I pushed that folder off to my right and slid the envelope with photographs to the front.

With a quick glance, it was easy to see that these were not official investigative photos taken by a deputy used to documenting a crime scene. It was obvious they were taken hurriedly by someone whose job did not require carefully shot and framed photographs. Still, they gave more or less adequate views of the Ferguson woman before she was moved, as she was being moved, and a few as if the photographer stepped back to take a few overall shots of the room as she was being loaded onto a collapsible gurney.

I looked at the eight-by-ten printout of Francine Ferguson as she was discovered. She lay on her back, just at the edge of the bed, so that her feet were flat on the floor, arms down by her side. She was completely nude.

Portions of firefighters' arms and bodies were at the edge of the picture as they had moved in to take her out of the house and the fire that was totally under control. Actually, it wasn't that much of a fire to start with. More smoke than anything. Most of the fire was near the front door, where the arsonist had started it with an accelerant. Later, the medical examiner determined there was no smoke in her lungs, although there had been plenty of smoke at the scene.

No abrasions or wounds were visible in that hastily shot photograph.

I flipped through other photographs and concentrated on the one taken as the woman was being moved. This one showed more of the overall room. The thing that struck me was the neatness. It didn't look like a crime scene where any sort of struggle had taken place. I've seen plenty of crime scenes over the years and this one didn't fit the typical.

My eyes were drawn to an upholstered chair near a shade-drawn window to the left of the foot of the bed.

Folded neatly on the chair were clothes the victim had apparently been wearing. I frowned. Clothes folded neatly?

Who the hell would fold their clothes and place them in a chair—before being raped and murdered?

Of course, there were plenty of reasons a woman might undress and leave her folded clothes on the chair by the bed. These looked somehow out of place, though, too perfectly aligned in comparison with the rest of the room.

I wanted to find out more about those clothes.

Chapter Three

I continued to ponder the folded clothes.

Did she know the person, and did she herself neatly put away her clothes in preparation for sex? Didn't seem likely. Not that methodically.

But if that were the case, it would certainly indicate she had no fear of what was to come after sex . . . or during sex. Still, no matter how casual sex had become, it didn't seem like a thing most women would do.

If it was indeed that casual, the act would point more to someone she knew, and knew very intimately. A steady boyfriend?

However, subsequent investigations had essentially eliminated a long-standing male friend.

And there was something about this killing that made Odell surmise that a serial rapist was involved.

I needed to see the more professionally made photographs from last night. Try to see what Odell had seen.

I pushed aside the pictures, slipping them back inside the envelope, and turned to the written reports and notes. Shuffling through the pages without concentrating on them, I stopped and took out the one photograph that showed the position of the Ferguson woman's body and the overall shot of the bedroom. Those damn folded clothes continued to pull my gaze, as if they glowed with a light of their own.

I didn't admonish myself for being so fixated on the clothes; I learned a long time ago that if something really bugged me, there almost always turned out to be a real reason for it, and a reason that bore fruit. Follow your instincts.

Trust them.

Taking a deep sigh, I leaned back in the straight-back chair, flexed my shoulders, and concentrated on actually reading the reports and notes.

I'm not sure how much time had elapsed until I heard the deep rumble of Balls' voice speaking to Mabel. The timbre of his voice reminded me of the way that powerful engine of his meticulously restored vintage Thunderbird sounded. Same deep tones. He used the Thunderbird as his official car as much as he could—unless it was an assignment that might put the vehicle in danger. Never mind if the mission put Balls in danger; but protect that precious Thunderbird, which next to his wife Lorraine and two grown children, he loved most in the world.

Mabel said something else to Balls. I couldn't understand what she said, but it must have been about my presence because in a few seconds the door to the interrogation room opened and Balls stepped in.

A half-grin on his face, he shook his head in mock disapproval. "A dead body. Might know you'd show up." Before I could respond, he made a face that signaled he wished he could change the words he'd just spoken. Glancing over his shoulder to make sure he was alone, he said more quietly, "Hell, I'm sounding like your good buddy Schweikert."

"Yep, good to see you too, Balls," I said.

He came around by my chair and hiked a hip onto the edge of the table, his concession to taking a seat. He looked at the file in front of me. "The Ferguson woman?"

"Yes."

He raised an eyebrow. "Odell think they're related?"

"Yes."

Balls sucked on his lower lip. Then he stood and said, "Going to pay my respects to the High Sheriff. Mabel says Odell will be back shortly." Putting his hand on the door, he studied something off in the far distance. "You guys keeping me busy here. I've got something that needs looking into down in Rodanthe, and then an active case up a little north of Duck, and now this one." He shook his head.

"See you at the press conference . . . or when Odell gets back."

He eased out the door and I turned back to the reports, but I didn't read any further right away. I began straitening up the pages, keeping them in chronological order. I figured I had time to run downstairs to speak to Elly before Odell returned.

An unusual quietness hung over the entire courthouse. That stillness was most obvious as I walked the hallway toward the front of the building and down the stairs. At the foot of the stairs, I stepped into Elly's office. Her coworker, Becky, aimed her round, cherubic face at me when I came to the counter. Her eyes were red-rimmed. She had been crying.

I spoke her name softly as a way of greeting.

Elly emerged from the small interoffice. She turned the hint of a smile in my direction, and she lightly touched Becky's shoulder with the fingers of one hand as she passed by her.

"Becky and Trigger were friends since grammar school," Elly said.

It was no surprise that word of Trigger Massey's killing had spread rapidly through the courthouse.

Elly wore a short-sleeved light pink cotton blouse and neatly tailored slacks. Her dark brown hair was pinned up in the back. Well, mostly pinned up. Always a few strands escaped and begged for me to kiss them against the back of her neck.

To Becky, I said, "I'm sorry."

"Thank you," she said, and busied herself straightening two of the large deed books.

"A press conference at one," I said to Elly. "I'll be there, of course. You?"

"If I can get away," she said.

"Meanwhile, I'll be upstairs with Odell and Agent

Twiddy."

"Already involved, huh?"

"Well, yes . . . yes."

She appeared emotionally to back off a bit. "Of course you are. I don't know why I said that. I'm sorry."

More power to her. In the past year or so she has accepted that I'm a crime writer, and that's what I do—I get involved. Took her a while to get used to the idea.

"I'd better get back on upstairs," I said.

Elly managed a smile, not a big one, but one filled with tenderness. I reached over and touched her hand and left.

I got upstairs as Odell came up the back way. Showered and shaved and in a fresh uniform, he looked like a different person. He nodded at me and then turned into the sheriff's office where Balls lounged back in one of the chairs too small for him.

I stood just inside the doorway.

As he eased himself out of the chair, Balls said, "We'll get out of your hair, Sheriff. Odell can fill me in."

Sheriff Albright said, "You two decided how much we say at the press conference?"

"Not too many specifics," Odell said. "Ongoing investigation. We'll try to get by with that as much as possible."

Albright nodded and made a note on a yellow pad on the desk in front of him.

The three of us went into the interrogation room. Odell took the single chair on the far side of the table. Balls and I sat next to each other. He inclined his head toward me and spoke to Odell. "Okay?"

"I have no problem," Odell said. "He's been going over the file on the other case . . ." With his chin, he indicated the Ferguson file on the table. I was lucky in that Odell accepted me as much as Balls did.

Balls sat relaxed, his fingers interlaced across his girth.

Odell flipped open a small spiral notebook and began. "We got the call at ten thirty-eight p.m. Call was made by a coworker—Karen Settle—who was working the evening shift." He named the restaurant, a relatively new one at the north end of Kitty Hawk. "The Massey woman had worked the day shift and this coworker, who lives down on Hatteras, sometimes stayed over at Trigger Massey's rather than drive all the way down to Hatteras late at night. She got there and found the victim, unresponsive in the bedroom. She called 911."

Balls raised the fingers on one hand, and Odell paused, waiting.

"Forced entry?" Balls asked.

"No, sir. Coworker didn't notice anything out of place when she entered through the unlocked front door, which was sometimes left open for her. A lamp was on in the living room. She didn't call out Trigger's name because she thought she might already be asleep. Walking past Trigger's bedroom to her own when she discovered the body."

That raised finger again.

Odell waited.

"Other than—I assume—checking the body for pulse, the coworker move her in any way?"

"No," Odell said. "She said she didn't even touch her. Just looked at her and called her name two or three times. Then 911."

Balls nodded.

"Units from Kitty Hawk, along with EMTs with the rescue squad, were the first responders." He checked his notebook. "We were there eighteen minutes later." He glanced at Balls and waited a moment. When Balls remained silent, Odell continued. "Medics didn't move the body. They're getting good at that. Checked for vitals they said. Left her like she was found."

"Photos?" Balls said.

"Oh, yes. Deputy Dorsey was right behind me, with his new camera the department bought him. Took a lot of pictures. A whole lot." He checked his watch. "Selected photos probably already on my computer, and he's printing out a couple dozen or so of hard copies. We'll look at those in a few minutes."

"Good." Balls said.

I, too, wanted to see those pictures. Check the condition of the room, especially the clothes.

"She was nude," Odell said. "And positioned like the other one—the Ferguson woman. Sitting with her hips on the edge of the bed, feet together on the floor, leaning back, with her arms down by her side."

"Wounds?"

"Nothing visible, except for a bruise on her left facial area. When Dr. Willis got there, he did a prelim. Indications were that she was manually strangled. Flecks of blood in her eyes."

"Sexual?"

"Probably raped, Willis said, but no visible evidence of semen." The slightest shake of his head. "Just like in the other one." He took a breath before continuing. "Dr. Willis said the autopsy would tell us more, including whether a condom was used—just like in the other one." Another quick look at the spiral notebook, and Odell told Balls about the aborted matchbook-and-cigarette incendiary device.

Balls straightened in his chair, did a quick arch of his back. "I gather you think it's the same perpetrator."

"I know, shouldn't jump to conclusions, but it's hard not to. I mean, no forced entry, body in the same position, nude, no real sign of a struggle, everything neat and orderly, half-ass attempt at a fire. Probably going to confirm manual strangulation, including fractured hyoid bone."

"Age?"

"Driver's license shows thirty-nine, almost forty. Old enough for the hyoid to . . . to firm up."

The tiny horseshoe-shaped hyoid bone in a youngster was so flexible it would not fracture during strangulation but would in a more mature adult.

Balls used his thumb and index finger to massage his moustache. "If the same perpetrator, then that more or less eliminates the usual 'person of interest'—the boyfriend."

Odell nodded. "That's my thinking." But then he added, "We'll check them out anyway. Especially Trigger Massey's because she had than more than one boyfriend."

Balls continued to run something through his mind. "No forced entry. Presumably known or trusted by both women. Permitted in. Maybe even welcomed." He sighed deeply and switched gears. "Okay, what in hell we gonna tell reporters at this . . . this press conference the sheriff says is set for one o'clock?"

Odell got a wry, half-smile. "You mean, aside from yes there's been a homicide, and the investigation is ongoing?" That half-smile disappeared. "Beyond that, damned if I know."

"Always fall back on awaiting results of an autopsy." As if it had just occurred to him, Balls said, "I assume Dr. Willis sent the body on to Greenville?"

"Yes, sir. Some hours ago now."

"Avoid any mention of a possible link between the two cases, including the fact that she was nude . . . and not sure yet about cause of death, other than evidence of foul play."

Odell nodded.

A tap on the door and Deputy Dorsey stuck his head in. Beaming proudly, he handed over an envelope to Odell. "Here're some printouts of scene photographs. More are on your computer."

Odell thanked Dorsey and took the envelope.

I wanted to see those photographs.

Chapter Four

Odell slid a stack of eight-by-ten crisp photographs out of the envelope. He glanced at the first one and handed it over to Balls. I could see it too. It was an overall shot of the room, taken apparently immediately upon coming onto the scene. Trigger's body was positioned as Odell had described.

Balls handed the photo to me without speaking. I studied it a bit longer and laid it on the table between the three of us. The next photo was a closer-up view of the body. Certainly no visible wounds, except what was probably that bruise on her face. She looked more like she was posing than murdered. Obviously, too, she hadn't gone along with the trend among younger women to shave everything from the neck down.

It took a moment for the impact to hit me: That this was a woman I knew who had just been murdered; that this was not playtime; this was for real. There had been that momentary disconnect between seeing the photograph of a woman posed on the edge of the bed and the reality of what I was looking at.

God, I never want to become immune to death.

I breathed in deeply and slowly through my nose and exhaled slowly from my mouth. I did that again. Then I laid the photograph down with the other one.

In the next photograph, taken from one side, the chair near the bed was clearly visible with her clothes neatly folded on the seat. With the photo in my hand, I spoke to Odell. "These clothes . . . you catalogue them or anything?"

He studied my face. Slowly, a smile began to creep upon

his lips. A knowing smile. "Yes . . ." he said and waited.

When I waited also, he added, "Yes . . . like the other ones, the ones at the Ferguson woman's house."

Balls cocked his head, first toward Odell and then toward me.

Odell said, "No one folds clothes like that right after being raped. And if the sex was consensual, what are the odds she'd fold her clothes the exact same way as Francine Ferguson? Either the killer did it, or he forced her to." He took a short breath. "We listed them . . . a cotton top, bra, shorts, and waitress shoes. You know, a little heavy duty."

Balls kept one eyebrow raised. "No panties?"

Odell shook his head. "Not in either set."

We were all three silent. Then Balls said, "Souvenirs?" He gave a short shake of his head. "Serial types have a tendency to want to take something to bring it all back to 'em. Jewelry maybe, but they kinda like get something more personal, more intimate."

"Yeah, I think souvenir," Odell said.

"Strengthens your theory about it being the same perpetrator," Balls said.

Odell nodded.

It surely seemed that way to me.

Balls again: "We got a serial rapist?"

"Afraid so. And a serial killer too."

Balls chewed on his lower lip. "No word at the press conference about souvenirs."

"Certainly not," Odell said. He glanced at his watch. "Maybe we better grab a bite to eat before . . ."

"Yeah," Balls said. "Go through the rest of the photographs first."

The remaining pictures didn't show anything we weren't already expecting. Odell slipped them back in the envelope and the three of us went across the street to Poor Richard's sandwich shop and sat near the rear.

I opted for a hot ham and cheese; Odell ordered a

Cuban; and Balls a Rueben, with extra fries. Sweetened iced tea all around. The food was in front of us in short order, delivered by a young woman in shorts, Poor Richard's T-shirt, scruffy sneakers, and short hair she appeared to have trouble controlling. A sheen of perspiration glistened on her forehead. But she graced us with a big, genuine smile, and said she hoped we enjoyed.

We ate silently at first. I wanted to talk a bit more about the case. So I said, "If both women more or less 'welcomed' the killer, doesn't that mean that it would behoove us to delve into acquaintances or contacts that were similar to both victims?"

With a mouthful of sandwich, Balls looked at me and said, "What's this 'behooves us' business and this 'delve into'? Hell, you sound like a writer or something."

Odell turned a smile toward his sandwich.

I shrugged.

Balls managed to swallow his food and said, "You're right, of course." He picked up a french fry with his fingers and pushed the plate toward Odell, who gave a tiny shake of his head. "Business people, services . . . and not someone who would arouse suspicion."

Playing devil's advocate, I said, "Or maybe someone they opened the door to, who then threatened them, maybe even with a gun. And gained access."

Odell said, "I've thought about that, too, especially since there was no indication at all of a struggle . . . beforehand."

"Service contracts. That sort of thing. We'll want to check," Balls said.

I thought about going over credit cards, but I didn't say anything.

After a while, Odell checked his watch and signaled the waitress for the check. Odell reached for his wallet.

But Balls put out a restraining hand on his arm. "Let Weav here get it. After all, we're letting him hang around with us, get material for more of his damn writing. Besides, he can write it off, probably.'"

Odell staged a mild protest, but I assured him I was pleased to do it—and that I was used to having Balls pull the 'you're paying' routine many times before. And I didn't resent it at all. We understood each other quite well after all these years. And sometimes he did pay, or we went Dutch.

After I had settled the bill, we went back across the street to the courthouse to get ready for the press conference.

Press conferences were held upstairs in the courtroom. Mabel had already placed a lectern at the front, and several chairs for reporters were arranged facing the lectern. I went up early and took a seat off to one side, away from the chairs that would be used by the daily news media. Balls and Odell were down that hall with Sheriff Albright, briefing him a bit more.

A couple of townspeople—courthouse regulars—came in and sat near the back. Linda Shackleford was the first reporter to arrive. We greeted each other with warm hugs.

She was one of the first people I met when moving to the Outer Banks. At that time, she was taking classifieds and obits for *The Coastland Times*. Then she became a photographer and later a reporter. She made real progress and developed into a good reporter. She moved on to the *Outer Banks Sentinel* as one of the top staffers until it folded, then came back to *The Coastland Times* as a lead writer.

Linda was also a good friend of Elly's. She was husky, with a great and generous grin that displayed large teeth I always said looked strong enough to chew through rawhide.

We chatted until a couple more reporters came in, and Linda moved over to take a seat up front. Jeff-something from Elizabeth City's *Daily Advance* arrived talking animatedly to Cheryl Darby with *The Virginian-Pilot*. Right behind them came one of the reporters for a Norfolk TV station; I recognized him but couldn't remember his name. He had a camera/soundman with him. They both hustled about busily, clipping a mic to the lectern, moving a couple of the chairs, with the reporter positioning himself so the shoulder-held camera could capture the anchor's profile and the lectern at the same time.

The other reporters watched them passively.

Shortly before one o'clock, Mary Ann Little of the *Camford Courier* took a seat, nodded to a couple of the other reporters. She worked for Thaddeus Sinclair, editor and publisher of the *Courier*, whom I had known back in the DC area when he worked for *The Washington Post*. Mary Ann was a widow with an almost grown son; she had gone back to newspapering a year or so ago and had written some extremely good in-depth pieces.

The excellent freelance journalist Kip Tabb hurried in, glanced about, and grabbed a seat. He was followed by two reporters who wrote for Outer Banks online publications.

Then I noticed that Gail Hutchison, the first appointee to the Sheriff Department's newly established post of Victims' Advocate, had come in and taken a seat right behind the reporters.

Standing against the wall by the rear door, Elly gave me a soft smile. I returned her smile, but then I saw Schweikert standing nearby. My smile faded. Schweikert glared in my direction, whether at me or simply in general, I wasn't sure. He glared a lot. That was his usual demeanor, as was his attire: a long-sleeved light blue dress shirt, precisely and sharply pressed. Courthouse talk was he didn't trust the laundry to do his shirts. Nor did he trust his wife; he ironed them himself.

Right on time, Sheriff Albright came in, followed by Odell and Balls, and went straight to the podium, keeping his eyes mostly down. He held a couple of yellow legal pad pages of notes. He smoothed those out in front of him on the lectern. Balls and Odell stood behind him a step or so, one to either side.

Then, for the first time, Albright looked up, a tentative smile on his lips as he nodded to the reporters. "Thank you for coming," he said.

And the press conference began.

Chapter Five

Sheriff Albright said, "I've got this brief statement to read for you." He paused, then said, "I expect, too, that this conference will be brief, because there's not . . . Well, let me read this."

Albright looked down at one of the yellow sheets and began reading as if giving a recitation in a classroom: "Last night at approximately ten-eighteen, we responded to a 911 call and went to a residence in Kill Devil Hills, where we discovered the body of a Caucasian female named Trikina 'Trigger' Massey. It was immediately determined that she was deceased. While I can't go into details yet at this time, there was evidence of foul play. It did not appear she had died of natural causes."

He cleared his throat. "At this time, no motive has been established and no arrests have been made."

With a short twist of his head, he indicated Odell and Balls. "The lead investigator on this case is Dare County Chief Deputy Odell Wright, assisted by Special Agent Ballsford Twiddy of the State Bureau of Investigations."

He swept his eyes across the group of reporters. "That concludes my statement. We'll take questions, and some I may refer to Deputy Wright or Agent Twiddy."

A flurry of questions erupted, one on top of another. Albright held up one hand. "We'll try to take these in some sort of order," he said. "Please." He pointed to Jeff of the *Daily Advance*, who wanted to know how the victim was killed. Albright danced around that question, as he would several others, by saying, "We're awaiting a full autopsy report from the medical examiner . . . but preliminary indications point to strangulation. There were no gunshot wounds or other obvious traumatic physical . . ." He appeared to search for a word. ". . . wounds to the body."

The TV anchorman, using his on-air voice, said, "While you said there have been no arrests, do you have persons of interest you'll be questioning?"

"Well, yes," Albright said, sounding a touch defensive, "We always talk with a lot of people in an investigation, but as far as naming anyone of 'special interest,' the answer is no."

The TV reporter followed up: "Sir, is that 'no' you have no one of special interest or 'no' you can't reveal the name of anyone?"

Odell stepped forward, which appeared to make Albright relax quite a bit. "What the sheriff is saying," Odell said, "is that, in all investigations, we talk with acquaintances, and especially the last person or persons to see the victim before the event. That doesn't mean that those people are necessarily 'persons of interest,' as the media has been inclined to label them, like they're under suspicion."

Albright quickly pointed to another reporter.

It was the woman from *The Virginian-Pilot*. "In addition to apparently being strangled, was she raped?"

Sheriff Albright cast a quick glance of appeal to Odell, who again moved forward a step or two. Odell said, "While there is some indication that sexual assault might have taken place, we must await the full autopsy report before we can say."

The reporter said, "What sort of 'indication,' sir?"

Odell appeared to struggle a moment with how to respond.

Balls stepped forward. "Anytime a woman is found slain, sexual assault is always one of the first things to be considered. That's what we are doing. Considering it. But we can't give you a definitive yes or no until we get the autopsy report."

"When will that be, sir?"

Sheriff Albright took over. "The medical examiner's office is giving this priority since it is an ongoing investigation of a situation that just occurred a few hours ago. To answer your question, probably by tomorrow."

Mary Ann Little raised her hand. "Was a rape kit used?" Mary Ann had recently written an in-depth two-part article on the development of the Sexual Assault Evidence Collection Kit, or so-called rape kit, and how it was being used effectively by various police departments.

Albright nodded to Odell, who said, "Since the body was being removed to the medical examiner's office right away, we determined there was no necessity to utilize a procedure with the Sexual Assault Evidence Collection Kit."

I almost smiled to myself hearing Odell sound so impressively professional and, yes, bureaucratic, with phrases like "no necessity to utilize a procedure." If it had been only the two of us talking, I'm sure we would have used more down-home language.

The sheriff didn't miss the opportunity to get in a plug for the newly acquired rape kit, and the creation of the Victims' Advocate post. I saw the smile on Gail Hutchison's face as Albright said, "Our Victims' Advocate, Gail Hutchison, is responsible for bringing us more up-to-date on different procedures. She made sure we had a rape kit." He paused a moment, formulating his words. "The rape kit is used mostly right at the scene. But in this instance, the body was transported to the medical examiner. The M.E. will perform the necessary . . . the necessary procedures."

More questions peppered the sheriff about the scene, whether there was forcible entry, the condition of the body, and whether another briefing would be held when the autopsy report came in. Albright managed to skirt around many of the questions. As to another briefing when the autopsy was available, he would make no promise.

Reporters had to be a bit frustrated with the briefing because they had only the bare basic facts—a woman was slain, her name, vague address, age, and no arrests or solid suspects. That was about it.

Reporters began shuffling out. The TV guy's cameraman retrieved the microphone from the lectern. I spoke again to Linda Shackleford and to Mary Ann Little, and I told her I had enjoyed her articles.

I glanced toward the rear. Elly had returned downstairs.

And Schweikert had disappeared, also.

I went back to the sheriff's office. He stood behind his desk, talking with Balls and Odell. I remained just inside the doorway.

Balls said to the sheriff, "That was relatively painless. You handled it well."

Albright looked down at the messages Mabel had placed on his desk. He acknowledged Balls' remark with the tiniest of smiles and a bob of his head.

"We'll get out of your hair now, Sheriff," Odell said.

Albright glanced quickly at Odell. "Been a long one for you, Odell. Get on home as soon as you can check out."

"Yes, sir."

I followed Balls and Odell into Odell's office. Odell sat behind his desk. Balls took one of the chairs, folded himself into it best he could, and I remained standing. Couldn't decide whether to sit. Maybe subconsciously, I wanted to be invited.

Odell watched Balls, who stared at folded hands in his lap, fingers intertwined. Great concentration on those fingers.

Odell waited. After a minute or so, he said, "Okay, what next?"

Balls didn't respond right away. Kept staring at those fingers. Then he let his fingers be and looked up at Odell.

"You know, same as I do, we start with the basics—those male friends of hers. Do that while a deputy checks with neighbors, who won't have seen anything but gotta be checked anyway."

I eased down onto the other chair, trying to remain invisible. I wanted to listen, and maybe add in a thought or two of my own if I believed I could get away with it. Technically of course, this was a police matter, and I had no legitimate right to be included; however, over the years Balls had certainly come to accept me, and now Odell did. In my prouder moments, I could convince myself that I was really part of the team.

Balls said, "I know you'll want a check if each woman had the same business or service contacts. Receipts, credit cards will tell." He sucked on a tooth. "Autopsy report'll be interesting, but I'll bet a nickel to a donut it doesn't show us anything we don't already know—manual strangulation, sexual intercourse with a guy using a condom." He gave a little tilt to his head. "Why the condom? DNA? Probably. And not a germ freak."

Odell listened. No surprises to him, I'm sure, but it always helps to get confirming input from others.

They were silent for a moment. An opportunity for me to slip in a word or two. "One thing we've talked about and sort of accepted," I said, "is that the killer was someone the women knew or trusted, which could explain the no forced entry. But another possibility it seems to me is that the women simply answered the door and the guy immediately intimidated them—with a gun, or knife or something—and then marched right in."

I took a breath, expecting a smart-alecky remark from Balls. He surprised me. "True," he said. "If he planned to kill them anyway, he didn't worry about whether they could ID him later."

Odell nodded his agreement.

Since I hadn't been shot down, I figured I could squeeze

in another observation. "I think we ought to look at both women, what they were like. Both about the same age, same coloration, medium brown hair, single, and most important probably is that both women had the same type personality—outgoing, friendly, but also rather fiercely independent. Women who asserted themselves. Friendly about it but assertive anyway."

I took a breath. "Maybe our rapist wants to take them down a peg or two." Another breath. "And I'll bet he will target the same kind next time."

I waited a moment.

Balls cocked his head at me. "You been reading those damn psychology books again?" He had difficulty hiding a smile.

Okay, the old smart-alecky Balls, my buddy, was back.

Odell spoke up. "That is interesting."

"Yeah, I know it is," Balls said. Quieter this time. "The guy does likely spend a lot of time picking out his target."

Odell said, "Almost feel like we ought to warn the public . . . or something."

Balls shook his head.

We were all silent for more than a minute. Then, taking a slightly different tack, Balls said, "Okay, he didn't get too serious about a fire this time. Next time—and there's going to be a next time, and maybe sooner rather than later—he won't even bother with a fire. He knows it doesn't work. Doesn't throw anyone off."

Odell said, "Sheriff's hoping there won't be a 'next time.' Good luck on that."

"Following the usual pattern, he'll get bolder. Unable to resist doing it again. Urge will be too strong," Balls said. "That's when we can hope he makes a mistake . . . before he gets too far with it."

Chapter Six

Before I left the courthouse that afternoon, I stopped by Elly's office. We promised that we would get together the next night. I looked forward to it. Being with her at her home, where she lived with her mother and young son Martin, was always so very comfortable.

I drove out of Manteo, across the Washington Baum Bridge at Roanoke Sound and headed up the Bypass through Nags Head toward Kill Devil Hills and my little blue house.

When I parked under my carport and cut the engine of my Outback, I sat thinking. There was rewriting I needed to do for Rose, my editor, but I couldn't unclutter my mind of this latest murder.

Trudging up the stairs on the side of the house, I entered through the kitchen and immediately Janey, my parakeet, began chattering away, welcoming me home. I spoke to her, opened her cage door to see if she wanted to come out. She didn't, which was not unusual. She was more of a homebody than some of the other parakeets I had had over the years. But she did enjoy my putting my hand in her cage to rub her head with my fingertip and let her nibble away.

During what was left of the afternoon and into the evening, I did get most of that rewriting done for Rose and sent it electronically to her in New York.

When I went to bed, I knew I was determined to get back over to the courthouse to see Odell and Balls early because I was confident the autopsy report would be in. At least a preliminary one. Too, I couldn't stop thrashing around different theories in my head about Trigger's murder. The fact that I knew her personally added to my obsession with the investigation, I'm sure. But as Elly can testify, I tend to get obsessed with ongoing investigations, gnawing over them like an old dog with a bone.

The next morning dawned clear and mild, light wind from the west. We had been having beautiful weather this spring. Oh, with a few sharp turnabouts, but no northeast storms or heavy rains. I took my coffee out on the deck and sat on one of the weathered wooden chairs. I'd secured a pad at the back of the chair so it was more comfortable sitting there. A great spot and time for coffee, an occasional cigar, and contemplation. Maybe some "pre-writing," as Elly called it.

I assumed Balls had gone home overnight but would be back this morning. He lived on the other side of Elizabeth City, slightly less than an hour from the Outer Banks, but at least an hour to Manteo.

Without bothering to call Odell, I decided to drive on to Manteo and the courthouse and simply show up. Too easy to say "nothing new" over the telephone.

Traffic was relatively light on the Bypass this early in spring. Gets pretty choked up during the season. We call Highway 158 the Bypass, even though the five-lane road bypasses nothing. Businesses, shops, and restaurants, including the usual fast-food places, crowd shoulder-to-shoulder on both sides of the highway.

At the top of the bridge over Roanoke Sound, the vast development of Pirates Cove marina and apartments, are off to the right. In the distance to the left but not visible is Wanchese, a boat-building area, unloading docks for fishing boats, and home to a good many Outer Bankers. A great place for locals and knowledgeable tourists to buy fresh-caught fish. Wanchese was the residence, too, of those with the fast-disappearing "hoigh toide" accent I love so much. Elly still has a trace of that accent on certain words.

By shortly after nine, I had parked on Sir Walter Raleigh

Street near Jamie's Downtown Books and the courthouse. Too early for the bookstore, but I would come back later, I was sure.

Going in the front of the courthouse, I passed Elly's office. She was busy talking with one of the paralegals from a local law firm. I raised a hand and caught a tiny bob of her head.

Upstairs, I met Odell as he left the sheriff's office and headed to his own. He gave a lopsided grin and ducked his head toward the door to his office. I followed him in.

"Got the prelim," he said. He referred to the autopsy report. He held up a couple of sheets of paper. Sitting at his desk, he began to read. Without saying anything, I quietly took one of the chairs to the side of his desk.

After a few minutes, I heard Mabel speak to someone in the hall. Then Balls' solid baritone rumble. Always made me think of his Thunderbird, as if the two were one and the same. He came into the office, dominating the doorway.

Odell looked up, spoke to Balls. "The prelim," he said.

"Good," Balls said, and took the other chair. He raised his chin and looked over at me. "You spend the night here?"

"Sure," I said. "But I dozed a bit in this chair. Wanted to be here when you finally got around to waking up and bringing yourself around."

A trace of a grin on Balls' face before he turned to Odell and waited.

Odell finished reading, probably for the second or third time. "Not much more than we knew or suspected. There was penetration, but no tearing or trauma. A condom was used. Evidence of spermicidal lubricant." He paused and checked something else on the report. "There was that bruise to the side of the head. Not clear whether that was made with a fist or a heavier object, but probably hard enough to cause at least partial loss of consciousness."

Balls rubbed his moustache, keeping his eyes on Odell.

"Manual strangulation, as we pretty well knew. No evidence of drugs ingested, or any needle marks. Blood alcohol normal." Odell chewed on his lip. "Report states victim was probably positioned postmortem."

Odell glanced up at Balls and then referred again to the report. "Now this is interesting. The fingernails of each hand had been cleaned underneath, like with a file or pocketknife blade. No residue with the exception of one microscopic bit of blue cotton cloth under one fingernail."

"The guy was sure as shit trying to rid the scene of any DNA," Balls said. "Condom, fingernails."

Odell said, "Yeah, with that attention to the fingernails, you gotta wonder if maybe she didn't manage to scratch him . . ."

". . . before he knocked her out," I said, "or killed her." Then silently admonished myself for jumping in with a thought.

Balls ignored my speaking out, and muttered to himself, "Not much evidence of any real struggle."

"The M.E. thinks the fingernails were cleaned post-mortem too," Odell added.

Balls went back to the struggle business. "Why wasn't there more evidence of resistance, like a fight there in the bedroom, or wrestling around, knocking stuff over? That sort of thing."

I chanced speaking up again. "Two reasons I can think of. Maybe that blow to the head was from the butt of a hand-gun, or maybe he had a gun or something like a knife to threaten her with, subdue her. Or maybe—and we know he is probably a neat freak from the way her clothes were fold-ed—he straightened up things after she was dead. That's when he positioned her on the bed like the other one. So maybe he also took time to make sure everything was all neat and tidy."

I waited.

Both Odell and Balls were silent. I was a little surprised they'd let me speak so much without interruption.

Balls nodded slowly. "Yes, those are possibilities. Would explain a lot." Then to Odell, "Anything else?"

"Not really," Odell said. "The full report—stomach contents, more technical stuff—will come later. But this, I believe, is the meat of it . . . for what it's worth and for what it tells us we hadn't already figured anyway."

"Checking the neighbors, anything?" Balls asked. His body language clearly indicated he didn't expect much.

Odell said, "I had a couple of deputies going door-to-door there yesterday. Of course, nobody sees anything. Oh, a couple of delivery trucks maybe. That sort of thing. But nothing of any help."

Balls sighed heavily, leaned back as much as the chair could bear. "Okay, Odell, you and me. Go talk with a couple of boyfriends." He looked over at me. "Me and Odell. Not you, sport."

"I understand," I said.

"You go talk to your sweetie. Leave the investigation to us big boys."

Odell shuffled papers on his desk, tried to hide the beginnings of a smile.

"Hey, that's a *great* idea, Balls," I said, as if the thought had suddenly occurred to me.

Actually, there were a couple of thoughts I wanted to pursue . . . in addition to speaking to Elly.

Chapter Seven

Among the follow-up I wanted to do was to talk at some length with Gail Hutchison, the sheriff department's Victims' Advocate, about the mind of a rapist. She would have a lot of insight, I believed, which would be helpful in profiling the type of person who might likely be a "person of interest."

Going downstairs I lucked out in finding Elly relatively free. She stood behind the counter. I leaned my arms on the counter. She stood as close as she could. She smelled great. Always like sunshine and fresh cotton.

"Lunch later?" I said.

"It'd be nice, Harrison, but I brought something from home. And you're coming over tonight to eat with us? Mother's expecting you."

Elly is one of the few people who call me by my first name. Most friends address me as "Weav."

I told her I looked forward to seeing her about six.

Then, with a lowered voice, even though there was no one around to hear us except her coworker Becky, she said, "The investigation? Any closer to finding out who raped and murdered poor Trigger?"

From the corner of my eye, I could see that Becky was trying to hear, while at the same time attempting to appear busy doing something else.

I shook my head. "Not yet." I wanted to change the subject. "Saturday night, Betsy and Debo are playing at Mulligan's. Want to go hear them? Grab a bite to eat there?"

"That could be fun," she said.

Betsy Robinson and Debo Cox played together as "Full

Circle." She was a favorite vocalist and had sung with the little jazz group I played with. She could really belt out a song. Debo, on guitar and vocals, could make a song come alive.

"What are you going to do now?" Elly asked.

Turning so I could quietly address Elly without her co-worker hearing, I said, "I would like to talk a bit with Gail Hutchison. Insight into . . . into this type of crime."

Elly nodded. "She's good. I wondered at the press conference if maybe she didn't want to have something to say."

"Maybe next time," I said. "I'm going to try to catch her before lunch."

I left the courthouse and headed a few doors down Budleigh Street to one of the temporary offices the county had in a small wooden building. That's where Gail was housed, at least for the time being. I was lucky. She was in and welcomed my dropping in unannounced.

Her office is small: an older wooden desk, file cabinet, two visitors' chairs, one somewhat more comfortable than the other. Gail is probably forty, trim and athletic. She wears her dark brown hair fairly long and has intensely penetrating green eyes, and a ready, genuine smile. It's the eyes that get you. Tiny crinkles are on each side. Rather than add age, they seem to make her appear almost ready to smile with kindness at any moment. No wonder victims feel comfortable with her. She came to the post with the department after several years as a volunteer on one of the sexual assault hotlines. She's still connected with the volunteers.

She flipped a palm at the more comfortable chair. "Please," she said.

I sat, returning her smile. We both eyed each other pleasantly. Then, a deep frown crossed her face, and she said, "It's horrible." She stared at the top of her desk for a moment before looking back at me. "So evil. So horribly evil."

Quietly, I said, "Yes."

"As if rape weren't bad enough . . ." Then, "But you

didn't come here for me to say how awful the act is. We both know that." A slight, questioning tilt of her head, those eyes crinkling with kindness. "So . . . ?"

"I want to get insight into the type of person who does this sort of thing. The rapist. Primarily the rapist." A weary, tiny shake of my head. "Unfortunately, I am familiar with the type of person who commits murder, although the variety of types does still astound me."

"Well," she said, "as you've probably read and heard many times before, it's not about sex. A sexual act, true, but not about sex in the way we normally think about the sex act, a passion in itself." She gave a rueful half-laugh. "And it most assuredly has nothing to do with romance."

She leaned forward, her forearms flat on the desk. "It's all about power. Brute power. The power to degrade, make a person submit. To violate."

I nodded. "What about when they are not . . . not raping? What sort of person? Appear normal? Married? A regular job?"

"Yes," she said. "Sometimes, all of the above. The rapist may have a regular job, be well respected. Yes, and maybe married—or have been married. A wife who may be cowed, or appear cowed, certainly." She raised one eyebrow. "Or maybe his ex-wife refused to be submissive. Subconsciously he wants to get even with her, so he rapes someone . . ."

I broke in, "Some*one*. With the emphasis on *one*."

"Yes," Gail said. "One. There may be only the one rape. However, if you track into his history, there were probably other times when it came close to rape. But the one act may be enough . . . and maybe he gets caught, or is afraid he'll be prosecuted."

I studied my folded hands a moment. "The rapist who does it more than once? The serial rapist . . . ?"

She pursed her lips in thought. "Yes, that worries me." She trained those eyes at me. "I'm afraid that's what we have. I've never seen that before. But I'm afraid that's what . . .

and that he'll do it again."

"And sooner?" I thought about what Odell had said earlier.

Lips still pursed, she nodded emphatically. "Sooner," she echoed.

We were both silent for one minute, two minutes. Then she said, "Another thing that worries me and that I think we have to assume is that this person may be one of us—one of the locals."

"Or a regular and frequent visitor," I said. "Someone who knows the area, chooses his targets carefully." Then I realized maybe I was talking too much. But I found her thinking quite good, and it sparked my own mind into whirling with possibilities.

After a while as we were winding down, I said, "Lunch? Can I buy you lunch?"

"Thanks," she said, "but I'm not hungry . . . and I'm going home early today. But thanks anyway for the offer."

I left her office and walked Budleigh Street the short distance to the courthouse, turned and headed toward Downtown Books. I was vaguely depressed. Maybe a visit in the bookstore would perk me up.

Walking with my head down, it didn't help my overall mood that I almost literally bumped into Schweikert. We both did startled double takes.

He gave a curt nod in my direction. "Weaver," he said.

"Schweikert," I responded, with the same tone of formality he had used.

He gave another curt movement of his head and continued on his way. As usual, he wore a long-sleeved, precisely ironed, dress shirt. This one was a pale yellow. Usually he favored light blue because, as one wag had said, Schweikert liked the way the blue brought out the color of his eyes.

Yes, that thought wormed its way quickly into my mind. That thought being the microscopic blue fabric found under Trigger's fingernail. From a long-sleeved dress shirt? One of

Schweikert's?

Aw, come on Harrison. No secret that you don't like him, but don't let this aversion creep into rational thinking.

Well, was it so irrational? After all, perhaps he did fit some of the characteristics that Gail Hutchison talked about. He did try to dominate, and he demonstrated traits of compulsive behavior, if his shirts were any examples. And I'd met his wife, who certainly appeared cowed by Schweikert.

I came to the door of Downtown Books, stopped, and pretended to be studying the beautiful Carolina blue sky with its sharply defined small white clouds. Actually, what I was doing was scolding myself for trying to make progress in an investigation by piling up non-existing evidence based on emotion rather than fact. Can be an occupational hazard for investigators, or a deterrent for enjoying blue skies and white clouds.

Okay, Harrison, get real.

Stepping into the bookstore, I breathed deeply. Loved that smell. Every business has its own distinct aroma, and a bookstore is about my favorite. Old newspaper offices, with the heavy smell of newsprint and ink, are right up there too. We won't even mention bakeries. No surprise that not among the favorites are funeral homes with their sickeningly heavy floral scent, and beauty shops of years ago when permanent wave solutions dominated.

But I was right at home in Downtown Books, and I touched my fingers lightly and practically unconsciously on a couple of new books on display near the door.

At the counter and cash register near the back, a young clerk, Evan, did something on a computer. He looked up and greeted me.

"Jamie?" I asked.

"She's up at Duck." He referred to Duck's Cottage, where she was the book buyer. "She'll be back here later this afternoon. Anything I can help you with?"

"Thanks, no. Just browsing."

"Make yourself at home."

I spent some time inspecting new releases. There are some good writers out there. A lot of them. Some people complain that they don't see how such-and-such a book gets published. Well, maybe some squeak by, but by and large I've been impressed, especially lately, with the quality of writing on the shelves.

Before I left, Evan asked me if I would sign a couple of copies of one of my books. Of course, I was delighted to do so. A true crime book, it's been doing quite well—keeping me happy, the bookstores happy, and most importantly the publisher happy.

Outside on the sidewalk, I breathed in deeply, and yes, the bookstore did boost my spirits.

I had stepped across the street to my car when I saw the Dare County Sheriff's Department cruiser coming slowly to the courthouse. Odell was driving. Balls was in the passenger's front seat. Behind them sat a tall youngish man I'd seen before.

I recognized him as one of the regulars at the latest restaurant where Trigger had worked.

A boyfriend of hers?

A person of interest, obviously, or Odell and Balls wouldn't be bringing him to the courthouse. Have a little chat with him. He must have been fairly nearby because not that much time had lapsed since I'd been with both of them inside the courthouse.

I stood there beside my car, hand gripping the door handle but not opening it. Damn, but I wanted to be there in the room when they questioned this guy. Frustrating. I couldn't be there, of course. Balls and Odell wouldn't take too kindly to my popping in. That didn't stop me from wanting—itching, aching—to be there.

Maybe late this afternoon I could drop by the courthouse and ask Odell if I could take a look at Trigger's financial records, see where she had been doing business and with whom.

He would tell me then whether the person they had brought in was actually a suspect, or whether he had managed to shed any light on the case.

Odell would do that much for me.

And Balls would probably be off on one of his other cases—either down on Hatteras or up in Duck.

Meanwhile, I would squirm a bit more but try to be patient.

Chapter Eight

Even though I wasn't hungry, I knew I needed to eat. After all, it would be a while before I could get back to the courthouse and try to find out something about the man Odell and Balls brought in.

Rather than leave Roanoke Island, I decided to eat right in Manteo. Darrell's, a long-time favorite of the locals, would be great. The parking lot in front was mostly full. I opted to park in back. The hostess led me to a small table on the right near the back. I could sit so I could see the people coming and going.

As I followed the hostess, I passed by the table of a friend of mine, Benny Baldwin. We both grinned at each other as a way of greeting. He continued listening attentively to one of the other two at his table, who appeared to be regaling them with a humorous happening of some sort. Benny's companions were employees of the town, I felt certain. Benny is a drone videographer—among other duties—and he does videos using a drone for all the municipalities in Dare County. They keep him busy. He does a lot of work, especially, for planning departments, getting a bird's eye view of land or neighborhoods. Weddings, too, and other special events.

He is excellent with drones. They behave like homing pigeons or trained and tame falcons with his delicate touch of controls.

For lunch I got a grilled cheese sandwich and tomato soup. And a second glass of water. I made myself eat slowly. Wanted to give Odell and Balls plenty of time. That worked out fine because when I was about two-thirds through, Benny and his group finished, and Benny spoke to the other two and tilted his head toward me, obviously saying he was going to speak to me.

He stepped close to my table. Because of a hefty bite of grilled cheese sandwich in my mouth, I didn't speak but pointed to the other chair at my table.

Benny pulled the chair out, sat, and said, "Don't want to interrupt your lunch."

"You're not," I said. "About through anyway."

Benny is maybe forty, tall and fit. He has a habit of rubbing a palm over his crown back and forth. Like many of us, he wore a collared cotton golf shirt and khaki slacks.

"I don't know what this area is coming to," he said. "Another woman gets murdered." He gave me a wry, half-grin. "I know your job takes you into a lot of murders, I suppose, but, you know, it's not something I can get used to."

"I understand," I said. "It is terrible, no two ways about it, and I'm not sure you ever get used to it." I waited. Took another small sip of soup, which was now only lukewarm.

He continued, as I knew he would. "It so happens that I was videoing up in Devil Hills the week before that first woman was killed. The Ferguson woman. And I was doing the area where she lived."

I put my spoon down.

"Yesterday afternoon," he said, "I was going through that video for something else and I realized I had a good shot of her house—the week before she was murdered."

A long shot, sure, but I asked anyway. I tried to make it sound casual. "Notice any activity around her house?"

"Yeah. There was a white service van in front of her house. You know, a panel truck with some writing on the side. Name of the business, I guess."

It was difficult to strive for a balance between sincere interest and a sense of growing excitement. I didn't want to overplay it—for my own sake as well as for Benny's. I didn't want him to think this was some sort of missing link, which, in all likelihood, it most assuredly was not. Still, it could have significance. Certainly worth looking into.

As evenly as I could, I said, "You remember that name of the business? What was written on the truck?"

"Naw, I didn't really pay any attention to it—and it was part of a long shot anyway."

"Could you zero in on the truck and maybe read the name?"

He looked at me and I could tell he knew this was important to me. That maybe he had stumbled onto something of real interest. "I'm sure I could," he said.

I fished in my wallet for a business card. "Call me on either my cell or landline if you can read the name of the business. I'd appreciate it."

"I'm headed back to the office. I know exactly where that video is. I'll zoom in on it soon as I get back. While I'm thinking of it." He rose from his chair. "Sorry to mess up your lunch."

I shrugged. "You didn't at all."

When Benny left, I pushed aside the soup and took one last small bite of the grilled cheese sandwich.

The waitress came up. She had a trace of concern on her countenance and in her tone. "Everything okay? You want something else?"

"No, no thanks. Not as hungry as I thought I was."

Her smile reappeared. "Gotta eat, hon. Keep your strength up."

I got the check, paid my bill, and stepped outside in the bright sunshine. We'd been lucky with the spring weather.

Retrieving my car, I drove back to the courthouse and parked. Sat there a while. I was in no hurry. Balls' Thunderbird was still parked in the same place, so he hadn't left to scurry off to Duck or to Hatteras. He had work in both areas, cases obviously part of his workload.

Starting to exit the car, my cell phone buzzed. It was

Benny. That was quick.

"I got right to it while I was still thinking of it," he said. "But no luck here in the office. I remember that particular video is archived at home. I'll check it later. Sorry."

No problem," I said.

Inside the courthouse, I went straight to Odell's office. He was not in there, but next door in the interrogation room with Balls and the man they had brought in. I could hear voices. It sounded as though they might be winding up.

I stood just inside the doorway to Odell's office so I could see out in the hall. The door to the interrogation room opened. Balls came out first, still talking over his shoulder. He was followed by Odell and the man they had been talking to.

The man was tall and lanky, with unusually long arms and big hands. Probably in his late thirties, maybe a hard forty. He wore a short-sleeved work shirt of some kind, not tucked in. He also wore a scowl. An intricate tattoo dominated his right forearm. He was handsome in a roughshod sort of way. His hair was thick and unruly. It didn't look like it had been combed this week, nor washed.

Odell said to him, "We know where to reach you if we need to talk more."

The man did not answer. He nodded. No smile.

"You need a ride?" Odell said.

"Naw. Just a couple blocks."

He'd probably been ready to walk a couple of miles rather than ride again as a reluctant passenger in one of the sheriff's cruisers.

The man went down the back stairs to Budleigh Street.

Balls sighed and shrugged his heavy shoulders.

To Balls, Odell said, "Not much, huh?"

"Probably not." He rubbed a big hand across his face. "I gotta get on up to Duck." Then, looking back at Odell, he said, "You an' me better get something a eat."

As if my presence registered on him for the first time, he

grumbled, "What you doing here?"

"Hanging around hoping you two had solved the case."

"Screw you," he said.

Odell, responding to what Balls had said to him a moment earlier, said, "I'm not really hungry. Hope to go home earlier today."

"I've already eaten," I said.

"Who asked you?" Balls growled, but barely able to hide the trace of a grin. "I'll grab something up in Duck," he added.

I faded a step or two into Odell's office while Balls and Odell made plans about when to get together tomorrow, and their next steps.

Balls left and Odell came slowly into his office and sank in the chair behind his desk. He studied an invisible spot on his desk. One hand pressed against the side of his face acted to prop up his head.

Silence from both of us. I could hear the solid click of each jerky second-hand spasm from a battery-operated wall clock in the office. Somewhere in the courthouse there was a distant, vague murmuring of voices.

After a full three minutes, I was the first to speak.

"Not much luck with the guy you and Balls interrogated?"

Odell made a face. Shook his head. He sighed, sat up a bit straighter. "His alibi was not all that solid, but . . ." He shook his head again. "We've got a couple more friends of Trigger Massey's we'll want to question. But . . ." Once again, his voice drifted off, tumbling with other thoughts.

I waited, hands folded in my lap, and studied Odell's face. Lines of weariness etched his forehead and cheeks. He turned his head and stared out the one window in his office, at the way sunlight seemed to mock the fact that we sat indoors. In profile, Odell has always reminded me of an ancient Roman coin that carried the image of one of the Caesars.

He turned back toward me. "We'll interrogate them, of course, along with anyone else we can dig up, but if my theory is correct, she wasn't the victim of one of her friends or acquaintances. Instead, she was the victim of the same serial killer and rapist as the Ferguson woman was—and we haven't got a connection between the two women, or any of their acquaintances."

I nodded but didn't say anything.

Silence again for a minute or two. Then Odell said, "I'll tell you, Weav, as if you didn't know, we don't have a single damn lead. Nothing. Nada. Zip. Zilch." He tried to fake a brave smile but didn't quite make it.

"I know," I said softly.

"So what do we do? We wait for him to strike again?" He bit at his lower lip. "Hoping we'll get luckier next time?"

Now it was my time to give a deep sigh, and I stood to leave, and I said, "I surely hope it doesn't come to that."

Chapter Nine

That evening, after showering and dressing in khakis and blue cotton golf shirt, boat shoes, I started the drive from my little blue house in Kill Devil Hills to Elly's on the west side of Manteo.

From the top of the Roanoke Sound bridge, I always enjoy the view ahead, especially like now in the late afternoon, early evening: The gleaming white boats crowd Pirates Cove Marina; Wanchese is no more than a vague hint off to the left; the trees on Roanoke Island silhouette black against the skyline; and the wetlands of heavy marsh grass spread out before me become the fur of an enormous sleeping animal.

I drove slowly through Manteo and continued out toward the airport and Fort Raleigh. Near the airport, I turned left off the highway and then another left later on, and pulled up in the driveway of Elly's house. Her mother's house, actually. Originally it was one of the Sears homes of the 1930s. But it has been modified and expanded so much over the years that except for the front view of the house, it's hardly recognizable as one of the Sears "you-build-it" home kits.

Their only neighbor is a single mom and her five- or six-year-old daughter Lauren, a close friend of Elly's son Martin.

A gigantic live oak tree, with its massive low, spreading limbs separates the two houses. The sandy ground under the tree has long been worn grassless because of play there by Martin and Lauren. Always, there are one or two toys—a miniature battered truck, an airplane, or a shoeless doll—at rest under the tree.

I cut the ignition on my car. Elly had come out on the front porch to greet me as I got out. Smiling, she waved wiggly fingers of an upheld hand. Martin stood sentry-like beside her. A year or two earlier he would have been hugging her leg. She had changed clothes and now wore knee-length tan shorts and a green short-sleeved blouse, flip-flops.

With an almost discreet light kiss on her upturned face, neither of us felt the need to speak. We grinned at each other. I did speak to Martin. He acknowledged my presence with a solemn nod of his head. That was more than he would have done in the not-too-distant past.

Inside, the living room always seemed so comfortable and homey. There was that one table lamp on at the end of the sofa, with a book on medieval history resting there, a bookmark visible a third of the way through the book. The latest crossword puzzle from *The Virginian-Pilot* and a ballpoint pen occupied a cushion on the sofa. Some of Martin's artwork, along with colored pencils, clustered together on the floor a couple of feet from the coffee table.

I breathed in deeply. "Supper smells great," I said. Whispering to Elly, I added, "So do you."

"You hungry?" she said.

With my corny Jack Nicholson leer, I said, "You make me hungry. Ready to eat."

A mock frown from Elly. "Behave."

Mrs. Pedersen, Elly's mother, came into the living room, drying her hands on a dishtowel. "Welcome," she said, with a wide smile. "We'll eat in about two shakes of a lamb's tail."

"Where does that phrase come from, I wonder?" Elly said.

"Huh?"

"Two shakes of a lamb's tail."

I chuckled. "Oh. We could ask Alexa or google it. But if you've ever seen lambs, sheep, standing around, they can twitch their tails faster than a dog can."

Martin huffed out a breath that smacked impatience. "Can we eat?" Apparently, he thought better of his tone of voice. He looked at his grandmother and added more softly, "If it's ready."

"It's ready. Come on, Martin," Mrs. Pedersen said. She is taller and bigger boned than Elly, who must have taken after her father. A Coast Guardsman, originally from Minnesota, he had been stationed at the Outer Banks where he met, courted, and later married the woman who would be Elly's mother.

Martin started to follow her into the dining room, stopped, and gave an exaggerated twitch of his rear. "Two shakes," he said.

Stifling chuckles, Elly and I followed them.

No wonder the food smelled so good. A plate of real North Carolina country ham centered the round dining room table. Wisps of heat wafted from the plate. A bowl of stewed corn also radiated. Cinnamon-topped applesauce glistened, and there was a slightly smaller bowl of green beans, a piece of ham fat visible among the beans. Of course, too, Mrs. Pedersen's made-from-scratch biscuits held a place of honor —right beside the butter dish and tiny pot of honey.

I made a mostly clumsy effort to appear positioning Elly's chair and helping her to her seat.

"Thank you, kind sir," she said. "Always the Southern gentleman."

I stood for a moment admiring the table. "My goodness, Mrs. Pedersen, this is all outstanding. I mean really. We should take a picture of . . . of this magnificent feast."

"Sit down and eat, Harrison," she said. (One other person who uses my full first name.)

As we ate, I complimented Mrs. Pedersen on the country ham. "Not over-cooked," I said. "Just right."

"Thank you," she said. "It's easy to over-cook—unless you remember to treat country ham the same way you would the white of an egg. Doesn't take much."

Elly said, "And mother puts a little water and a pinch of sugar in a frying pan and brings that boiling almost to a slurry, or syrup, before plopping the ham in for forty-five seconds or so on each side—and voila! It's done."

Smiling, Mrs. Pedersen passed me the green beans. "She's giving away my secrets."

While we adults ate some of each dish, we did limit ourselves to rather small portions.

For dessert, Martin had a small dish of vanilla ice cream. The rest of us declined. Well, I did make a dessert for myself with another biscuit and butter whipped with honey.

Afterward, Elly and I offered to help with the cleanup but Mrs. Pedersen, as expected, would have no part of that.

Martin sprawled out on the living room floor with his artwork. The night was balmy enough that Elly and I opted for the two-person swing on the front porch. The supporting chains creaked a comforting welcome as we gently rocked back and forth.

A minute, two minutes passed before either of us spoke.

Elly was the first to express thoughts along the line I know both of us mulled over. "No progress on Trigger's case? Or the Ferguson woman?"

"Not a thing," I said. "Odell's pretty frustrated."

"Agent Twiddy helping him?" Elly steadfastly refused to call him Balls.

"To the extent he can. He's got a couple of other cases in the area I know he's having to work on."

"Mabel says there's one up at Duck involving drugs coming down from Sand Bridge. The Virginia area that she says could be big—and dangerous."

"Mabel knows everything."

"She surely does that."

"Balls hasn't said anything about it. Not to me. Not yet."

We were quiet again. The night air smelled good. Daytime sun had warmed nearby pine trees and I could smell them breathing out their aroma. I rocked our swing gently and listened again to the chains that held us. As friendly a sound as if they were crickets.

I sensed we both welcomed another topic.

"Looking forward to hearing Betsy and Debo on Saturday night," I said.

Elly put her hand on my arm. "Oh, me too. That'll be fun."

We were able to not talk about murder until it was almost time for me to go and for Elly to get Martin ready for bed.

Then she said, "I hope there's not another one. Women I know are getting scared."

"I certainly hope there won't be too." Then I lied, betraying what I really thought. "And there probably won't be."

When I got home there was a message on my machine from Benny Baldwin. I clicked on play.

His voice came through with enthusiasm. "When I pulled up the video I shot that day, I was able to zoom right in on the Ferguson woman's house and that work van out front. The name on the truck was 'Bugs Away.' A pest control company shortly across the bridge in Point Harbor." He gave me a phone number. An easy one to remember, and I'm good at remembering numbers, but I jotted it down.

Now the next thing I wanted to do was to check Trigger's credit cards, home bills, see if perhaps—just perhaps—she had used the same pest control company. No sense in getting optimistic about this, I told myself. Surely, too, I didn't want to say anything to Odell or Balls about looking for a connection. Too farfetched. Just the same . . .

I went to bed to read, as always, but I did feel a bit more upbeat because at the very least there was a glimmer of something to look for.

Chapter Ten

Friday morning, I uncovered Janey's cage as I went into the kitchen to fix coffee. She didn't chirp for the first minute or so. Like all of us as the years go by, it usually takes her a little while to come around first thing in the morning. But by the time my Keurig groaned out a cup of coffee for me, Janey was fully awake and chirping excitedly. She loves activity.

Before nine o'clock, I was on my way to Manteo and the sheriff's office to take a look at Trigger's credit card bills and home maintenance records. I figured if Odell didn't already have them in his office, there'd be no problem for a deputy to retrieve them from her house which was secured with yellow and black crime scene tape.

I stopped at the Quality gas station on the causeway to fill up my Outback with fuel, and then I stopped again at the Dunkin' Donut shop as I came into Manteo. A half-dozen assorted donuts might be appreciated.

Elly must have been in the small interoffice because I didn't see her as I came into the courthouse, bearing my donuts—and a slim, spiral reporter's notepad and pen. I went right upstairs and headed to Odell's office.

But he wasn't there.

A light was visible from the partially opened door of the interrogation room. Figuring he might be in there with the file folders spread out for study, I popped right in.

Yes, there was someone there, but it wasn't Odell. It was J.R. Phillips, a female deputy. She sat in the chair on the other side of the table, facing the door.

She looked up at me. Face blank. That cop stare, revealing nothing, except maybe a slight defensive suspicion—of everyone.

Somewhat flustered, I held out the box of donuts like an offering. "Want a donut, J.R.?"

Her voice dead level, she said, "Are you one of those who think that the only thing that cops eat are donuts, Mr. Weaver?"

Did I really detect the tiniest hint of amusement at the corners of her mouth and in those cop eyes?

With exaggerated bravado, I opened the box and took one of the cinnamon sugar ones and bit down on it heartily. I took a seat opposite her. "It's Weav, J.R., no Mister."

I had met her on an earlier investigation and was impressed with her skills and professionalism. Obviously, Odell was too because he has been bringing her in on investigations, grooming her. She had been enrolled in a community college taking courses in criminal justice. Maybe she was already pursuing a degree at a four-year institution.

Probably in her late twenties, she wears her hair rather short, brushed back at the sides. Erect posture, shoulders back. Flat stomach. No nonsense. But if she's trying, she can't hide the fact that she's a pretty female, and all woman.

She had discreetly closed the folder she had been studying when I barged in. But she did manage something of a smile and held one hand out toward the donut box. "I will take one of those . . . Weav. Thanks."

I pushed the box across the table to her. "Sorry to interrupt you like I did. I was looking for Odell. Thought he was in here."

"He and your bud . . . he and Agent Twiddy are . . . are out."

She almost said "your buddy." I didn't expect her to tell me where they were or what they were doing. Probably, though, interrogating other friends and romantic acquaintances of Trigger's.

I nodded. "I'll leave the donuts here," I said.

"They won't last long." J.R. actually smiled. She was really pretty, despite herself.

I went downstairs but Elly was busy with two paralegals, so I waved and mouthed, "I'll call you."

She managed a nod of response.

I felt sort of at loose ends, as they say. Felt like I struck out. Well, I had. I wanted to go over those household bills and receipts of Trigger's. But let's face it, that was probably no more than busy-work. You don't solve a murder investigation that simply. The off chance that Trigger and the Ferguson woman used the same pest control company that was somehow involved in the rape and slaying of both women was . . . was, well, less than slim. My driving over here with that purpose in mind bordered on laughable.

That was an exercise I could put off until I had nothing else to do. And it was not as if I had nothing else to do. First of all, I needed to call Rose, my editor in New York. I keep her apprised of anything I'm working on, and she and I have been fortunate over the years, with articles, three books, one of which was used as the basis for a made-for-TV movie. That proved to be lucrative for Rose and for me—and I wanted to keep Rose happy and prosperous. A bit of enlightened self-interest.

I decided to wait until I got back home to call Rose because she had hinted that she had an editing job she hoped I would accept. I wanted to be sitting at my desk and have pencil and paper ready to make notes. An editing job did not excite me, but one must sometimes make sacrifices.

When I got home and called her, the first thing she said in her strong Brooklyn accent was, "Well, Weav, how are things down there in Magnoliaville—the land of mint juleps, murder and mayhem?" Then she cackled out a laugh and cigarette-induced cough.

I like Rose.

I told her about the latest rape and murder and the fact

that it appeared we had a serial rapist/killer in our midst. She could barely conceal her enthusiasm for another story.

"Meantime, Weav, I hope you'll do a bit of an editing/rewrite job for me."

"What you got, Rose?"

"What I've got is a mess. An article one of the biggies wants. And it's a good confessional and exposé piece, but the writing is—well, the writing is shitty." She told me the name of the author, a well-known television and movie personality.

Of course, I agreed to do it. She told me what she would be able to pay, and it was ample.

"Get it by midweek?" she asked.

"I'll try, Rose. Send it to me, and I'll see how much work is required."

"Counting on you, Mister Southern Gentleman. You're about the best editing/rewrite/writer I've got."

"What do you mean, 'about the best'? I *am* the best."

That cackle of a laugh again. "Well, yes, you are. Wanted to see if that streak of Hemingway-competitive-nature was still intact . . . or whether that soft beach living has gotten to you."

A bit more banter between us and then we signed off. Within a few minutes, an attachment icon appeared in a message from Rose. I opened the article and glanced through it. I could see why she said the writing was shitty, but I could also see how fascinating the story was. The tell-all aspect would make a number of high-profile individuals cringe with humiliation and embarrassment. Probably be some lawsuits —but that would not be my problem, and probably not Rose's either, I hoped.

I checked my calendar for the next day—Saturday. Clear. I would be able to work on the rewrite two or three hours or more. About my limit. Then that night Elly and I would go to Mulligan's to hear Betsy Robinson and Debo Cox. I looked forward to that.

Later on that afternoon, I got a call from Elly. I was puzzled and maybe vaguely apprehensive because she was still at the office and rarely initiated a call to me during working hours.

She spoke softly. "You be home this evening?"

"Yes. What's up? Everything okay?"

"Oh, yes," she said. Her voice became a whisper. "Something interesting I want to talk over with you, over the phone but not here." She wouldn't tell me what it was about. Not even a hint, other than to say it was something she knew I would find fascinating, and maybe even helpful. She said she would call as soon as she got home.

"I'm most eager," I said.

And I was.

I kept checking the time. That afternoon seemed to drag out. Maybe a trip to the nearby Food Lion, pick up a few things, would help move the day along.

By four o'clock, I was busy in my kitchen fixing a rather lavish fruit salad. I would have that and maybe a grilled cheese sandwich. I was hungry, or rather weak, because I realized at some point during the late afternoon I hadn't eaten lunch. I vowed to do better than that.

I pushed the mostly made fruit salad aside and took my seat in the little chair by the phone. It was about time for Elly to call. Right at five-thirty my phone rang. It was Elly. She was home and spoke in a more normal tone of voice.

"Okay, sweetheart," I said. "I've been awaiting your call."

"I'm sure you have, and I'm sorry I couldn't talk earlier but . . ."

"I understand," I said.

"Well, I had a most interesting conversation—at least I think it was a conversation, even though pretty one-side—with Karen Settle."

"Who?" The name sparked an elusive bit of memory, but I couldn't quite recall.

"Karen Settle, the woman who lives—or lived—sometimes with Trigger. The woman who found Trigger."

"Oh, yes." I could picture her now: short and tiny, but appearing taller because of erect posture and broader shoulders than expected; medium blonde hair, long enough to touch her collar, mid-twenties or so.

"She came by the Register of Deeds this afternoon. She said her two brothers wanted her to find out who owns the house Trigger lived in. She said—or claimed—that her brothers had said something about trying to buy the house for her." A slight pause from Elly. "But to tell the truth, that may have been partly the reason she came by, but I got the sense right off the start that there was something else she really wanted to talk about. She sort of delayed, and I gave her a piece of paper to write down information about the house, and that Jim Perry Realty owns it."

I listened intently. I knew there was more.

"Then, Harrison, Karen took a big breath and looked at me right in the face for the first time and said, 'Aren't you the friend—girlfriend—of Mr. Weaver? Harrison Weaver? The writer.' And of course I said I was."

"I'm glad you are . . . and I know you wanted her to . . ."

"Yes, I wanted her to go on. I knew she had something else to say, and I knew it wasn't about buying that house. She said, 'I've been told Mr. Weaver knows how to keep a secret. I mean he knows *when* to keep a secret. That he can be trusted not to say something, you know, at the wrong time.'"

In the background I heard Martin trying to get his mother's attention. "Just a minute, Martin. Mama's on the phone now."

Back to me, she said, "Sorry." Then, "Karen went on to say that she knew the police had been talking to boyfriends of Trigger's."

Elly paused a beat or two before continuing. "I had kept mostly quiet to let her go on talking." She breathed out a tiny chuckle. "I followed your advice about interviews, Harrison —that if you keep quiet long enough the other person will fill in the void by running on at the mouth. What is it you say, nature doesn't like a vacuum?"

"Yes, yes . . ." I said. I was eager to move it along.

"Karen said the thing she had been building up to say, and something she obviously wants you to know."

I gripped the handset hard against my ear.

"Karen said, 'Trigger was seeing someone nobody knows about. And that worries me. Who it is. Scares me.'"

Chapter Eleven

"Who?" I blurted out. "What did she . . ."

"That's just it, Harrison. She wouldn't say. Wouldn't tell me. She will tell you, I'm sure. In private. She was very nervous. Well, maybe not nervous nervous, but certainly ill at ease. Laying the groundwork to talk with you."

"When?" I tried to have my voice more under control, more reasonable sounding.

"I told her that I knew you'd like to talk with her," Elly said, "and I emphasized how discreet you could be and not say things that shouldn't be said . . ."

"But when?"

Elly's voice became tinged with irritation. "Stop interrupting me, Harrison."

"Sorry," I said.

"She said Monday."

"Jeeze. Not until then? Why not . . ."

"She said she would not be available at all until Monday. I pushed her as much as I could."

I tried to sound more reasonable. "I'm sure you did."

"I *did*, Harrison."

"Sorry. I meant it. I know you did."

"Mama will be right there in a minute, Martin."

"I know you're busy now, Elly, and I'm sorry if I sound . . . sound pushy. Don't mean to." I know she could hear me take a deep breath. "But . . . here it is Friday afternoon. Seems like Monday's a long way away."

"She said she would be working the early shift Monday at the Dunes and would be able to talk with you after the lunch crowd clears out."

"If she doesn't get cold feet by then . . ."

"Knowing you, Harrison, you'll be able to sweet talk her into warming her feet up again."

I thanked Elly and told her how much I appreciated it. And I did. I really did. I know I can be a pain at times. Elly knows that too, and she lets me know.

I heard her speaking to Martin as we signed off.

So, still sitting there by the phone, I mentally played around with that bit of intelligence. And it was only a tiny bit of intelligence. I shouldn't get all that excited. But *was* it only a tiny bit? Maybe it was something that could unlock the case. Yeah, right. Just like that.

I got up and went to my workstation—the dinette table cum desk and computer, printer, and file cabinet. Doing the best I could to clear my mind of Karen Settle's conversation to Elly, I printed out the article Rose had sent me as an attachment.

As I got into the work, and tried to fix some of that shitty writing, my mind did shift to the task at hand, and I managed to stow away my anxiety over wanting to know who the mystery visitor was who came to see Trigger—in secret.

By late afternoon I'd made more progress on the rewrite than I expected. I closed my computer, rubbed the heels of my palms against my eyes, and leaned back in the chair, trying to ease the back muscles. Almost time to take a long hot shower.

I didn't work any more that evening, but I did get to it fairly early on Saturday morning and spent much of the day at it. I could see that by late Sunday I should be able to send the edited copy back to Rose and surprise her with it Monday morning when she struggled into work.

Time to get ready for my Saturday night date with Elly. I looked forward to seeing her and going to Mulligan's.

At seven o'clock I pulled into Elly's gravel driveway. Going to the front door, which stood ajar, I called out a hello, and stepped inside at the shouted "Come on in" from Elly.

Martin came into the living room with one of his drawings in hand. As usual, he studied me solemnly. But when I spoke to him and knelt beside him, he got a barely held-back smile.

From the back of the house, Elly called, "Be out in a minute or two."

"No rush," I said. "Martin and I are visiting. I think maybe he'll show me his artwork."

Now Martin did smile. He handed me the drawing, done on a stiff piece of off-white cardboard. It was another scene of the live oak tree playground between their two houses, his and Lauren's. And it was excellent, even better than the last one he had done. Most children his age drew trees that looked more like lollipops than trees. His was leafy and airy, branches clearly visible, artfully placed leaves. Underneath the tree were a couple of toys—that beat-up truck on its side, a stuffed doll with arms and legs askew.

"My goodness, Martin this is *really* good. Really." I called to Elly. "He's getting better and better. A lot of talent." And it was true. The lad had the makings of a first-class artist.

Mrs. Pedersen stuck her head in from the dining room/kitchen area. "He is getting good, isn't he?"

"He certainly is." I stood. "And how are you, Mrs. Pedersen?"

She said she was fine and that she hoped we'd have a good time tonight. Elly came into the living room. She beamed a hello and touched Martin gently on the head. Elly wore trim slacks—and she wore them well—and a soft blue buttoned blouse. A lightweight cotton sweater was draped across one arm. She smelled good.

To her mother, Elly said, "It'll be rather late when we get back."

"Fine," Mrs. Pedersen said. With a half-smile, she added, "Remember we'll leave early in the morning for Greenville. You won't be able to sleep in."

Elly returned the smile and tilted her head toward Martin, "I never can."

Once a month, Elly and her mother and Martin drove the two hours or so to Greenville to spend Sunday with Mrs. Pedersen's older sister, who was in poor health and lived alone.

After the usual reassurances to Martin, and even a promise from Mrs. Pedersen that Martin was in for a treat, Elly and I made our departure. We drove through Manteo and swung left toward the Roanoke Sound bridge and Nags Head.

Mulligan's was on the east side of the Bypass in Nags Head. A colorful orange paint job made the two-story structure stand out vividly. At least I think it's orange. Like many men, I'm not that great on colors.

The hostess at Mulligan's was all smiles and I told her we'd like to sit upstairs and as close to the music as possible.

"Oh, they're good," the young woman gushed. We followed her up the back stairs and she seated us against the wall, only a place or two away from where Debo and Betsy would perform. They weren't on for another fifteen or twenty minutes. The upstairs, with its bar and tables, and an ocean view, was already becoming crowded. "Full Circle," the name of Debo and Betsy's musical duo, was popular—and it was, after all, a balmy Saturday night in the spring, and at the Outer Banks. Life was good. What more could we ask for? It was so good that I had—at least temporarily—not thought about murder and mayhem, and a serial rapist.

Food was not the foremost on our thoughts. We ordered a salad we'd split, with balsamic vinaigrette dressing on the side, a couple of club sandwiches, knowing we'd never be able to finish them. Could always take leftovers home. Certainly not above doing that.

We were toying with our food when Betsy and Debo began squeezing into their tucked-away area. Then they saw Elly and me as I stood to greet them. I maneuvered out from our table and shook Debo's hand. Gave him a clumsy hug and a full-blown hug for Betsy. She even planted a big kiss on my cheek. Other customers greeted them with applause.

They kicked off the music with a rousing rendition of "Two More Bottles of Wine." It was fun listening to them. Betsy could really belt out a song. A few numbers later she did a great version of "Blue Bayou." Debo backed her up with his guitar and a pre-recorded rhythm section that played on an amplifier beside him. They did "Ticket to Ride," and I could hear some patrons singing along with them.

They played one tune after another, some of which were requests shouted out by customers. A couple of waitresses scurried back and forth with beer orders.

During a temporary lull, Elly leaned close to me and said, "Why don't you make that request?"

I paused only a moment. "Okay." I wormed my way out from our table past the couple sitting next to us and leaned over close to a smiling Betsy. A trace of perspiration glistened on her upper lip.

"Betsy," I said, "this is my father's birthday. I wonder if you'd play his favorite song." I had my hand on her shoulder. It felt warm. I tilted my head heavenward. "He's up there somewhere and he'll hear it."

"Of course, Weav. I think I know what it is because you told me once before."

"Yes, I said. 'Danny Boy.'"

By the time I'd taken my seat back beside Elly, Betsy announced, "And now by special request from a very special dear friend—and writer and fine bass player—we're going to do 'Danny Boy,' his late father's favorite piece."

The crowd grew quieter, and as she sang, with her heart so into the familiar melody and the touching lyrics, a silence spread throughout the second floor.

I couldn't help it. The lyrics and the melody brought back such memories. I could see him sitting there with his ever-present cigar, the sadness in his eyes, listening to my mother sing and softly accompany herself on the piano. They were both gone now, but I knew they were listening. My eyes began to tear up. Elly gently placed her hand on my forearm and let it rest there, after a tender squeeze.

And then Betsy got to the lines that really do me in:

When winter's come and all the flow'rs are dying,
And I am dead, as dead I well may be,
You'll come and find the place where I am lying
And kneel and say an "Ave" there for me.

But I shall hear, though soft you tread above me,
And all my grave shall warmer, sweeter be.
And you will bend and tell me that you love me;
And I shall sleep in peace until you come to me.

With the back of my free hand, I had to brush away at my cheek. When Betsy finished, the entire place was hushed —for a moment or two. And then the applause was loud and enthusiastic. I looked at Betsy and silently mouthed "Thank you."

Debo took the microphone and said, "And now for a change of pace, we'll rock 'n' roll with . . ." and he named a tune I wasn't familiar with, but it was bouncy and upbeat, and I was happy for that.

Shortly after nine, Betsy and Debo took a break. Elly and I spoke to them, and I told Betsy that we'd have to be leaving soon because Elly had an early morning departure. Well, that was true, to an extent, but what I really wanted to do, and I was hoping that Elly also favored my deviousness, was to drive up to my little house for intimate time by ourselves.

We drove to Kill Devil Hills mostly in silence. Elly

briefly rested her hand on my forearm. I glanced at her and smiled. She returned the smile. At my house, I pulled in under the carport and I came around to the passenger side to open the door for her. She had already opened it, but she smiled again and said, "Thank you, kind sir."

We went up the outside stairs and into the kitchen area. Janey started chirping as soon as she heard us. She bobbed her head in greeting.

Elly said, "Hello, Janey. You going to be nicer to me tonight?"

Clear as anything you ever heard, Janey chirped, "Bitch."

"Same to you, Janey," Elly said, her face close to the cage.

Even though female parakeets rarely mimic words, Janey did two words perfectly. She had used half of her vocabulary greeting Elly. The other half of her vocabulary consisted of the word "shit." I know she picked up both of those words from me as I spent probably hours practicing a particularly tricky bass part on Mozart's "Requiem."

"Ignore her," I said to Elly.

She and I stood there a little awkwardly for a moment or two, until we embraced. We did that with a hunger. I took her hand, and we went into the bedroom. I had left a soft light on in a lamp on the far side of the bed.

Elly looked at the lamp. She got that slightly mocking half-smile going. "Cozy, Harrison," she said.

"I've even got fresh sheets on the bed," I said.

"We'll pretend we're back in Paris," she said, referring to the trip we'd made back to the City of Light a few months earlier. I knew she thought about the double bed we had in the apartment there.

I came closer and began to unbutton the top of her blouse. She said, "Let me help you," and began undoing the buttons and removing the blouse, and then the slacks, and bra, and little blue cotton panties. I watched her and admired her, and I said, "You're lovely. Absolutely lovely."

She went to the bed and pulled back the spread. "And you, sir?"

"Oh," I said. I began to undress quickly. "So captivated looking at you . . ." In a few seconds I tossed my clothes toward the chair near the foot of the bed. Most of her clothes had made it there, too.

Elly was in a playful, happy mood. She was stretched out but propped up on one elbow. To me, she looked like a painting, the reclining nude. With one eyebrow raised, she grinned, staring at me as I approached her. "Why do I think about Paris—and especially the Eiffel Tower—at a time like this?"

"You're naughty," I said.

"And you're impressive," she said.

"All because of you."

We held each other and squeezed tightly together. I could feel her breathing and I know she could feel me breathing too.

We were totally together now and in a short while she started saying, "Oh, oh, oh, oh . . ." She said it quietly but with an urgency. And she kept repeating it a while longer. Then we lay there, and I think both of us were smiling.

A little while later, we stirred out of bed. Elly gathered a few of her clothes and went to the bathroom. I called to her that I had laid out a fresh towel and bath cloth for her. She spoke loudly, "You've thought of everything, dear sir."

"There's even that hand lotion from Paris that we bought. Out there for you if you want to use it."

I was mostly dressed when she came out of the bathroom and started putting on her slacks. They had slipped off the chair and onto the floor. I had intended to pick them up before she came out.

Then, like a switch being flipped, pictures of the neatly stacked clothes at the rape scenes came to my mind. Immediately memory transported me from now to those pictures.

Elly was watching my face. "What's the matter."

"Oh," I said, with a quick smile. "Nothing. Thinking about something . . . something that has nothing to do with us."

"The rape and murder investigation?"

"You know me too well," I said, trying to sound jovial. Not sure I pulled it off.

She pulled her slacks up and fastened them, slipped her feet into her flip-flops. "Maybe Monday you'll find out something from Karen Settle that will help."

"Well, maybe," I said. ". . . maybe, just maybe."

Chapter Twelve

All day Sunday it seemed like Monday would never come. I forced myself to put the finishing touches on the rewrite job of that article for Rose. I went through it again from start to finish. Made a half dozen additional minor edits.

Actually, now it read pretty well. I figured the publication would have their lawyers go over it—at least they damn well better because some of those high-profile celebrities mentioned in the article would be out for blood.

I vowed to take one last look at the article by late afternoon before sending it as an attachment to Rose. In the meantime, the ocean beckoned. My sanctuary. My place of reverence and reflection—the ocean, and its vastness, and its unimaginable and totally ungovernable power.

Driving south on the Bypass, I turned onto Ocean Bay Boulevard and parked at the beach access lot at the end of the road. A fancy name for a road that is one block long.

Only five other cars were in the paved parking area. I strolled up the long wooden walkway toward the ocean. I could smell the ocean in the air, a slightly female aroma, and I could certainly hear it, the ceaseless roiling of the surf as it chewed up the beach sand and then redeposited it up and down the coast.

At the top of the walkway, I leaned against a railing and watched the ocean, studied it, marveled at it. I stared out to sea, as far as my sight would take me, to where the sky and the ocean came together. Some days they blended together so closely that they became one. Other days, like today, there was a sharp line between the sky and the end of the ocean.

At least it was the end of the ocean as far as my eye could journey. Watching that ocean, though, I thought about how it would be if your sight would keep going and going and going—and then, eventually, you would come upon the sandy and rock-strewn beaches of North Africa. Not Europe, but North Africa. That's what lay across that vastness directly to the east of where I stood.

I'm not sure how long I stood there. I was alone, and that was nice. When I finally decided to leave and started retracing my steps along the wooden walkway, I met an older couple coming toward me. He had a short gray beard, and she had a beautiful face, large brown eyes, and a full head of curly gray hair. Her hair was very pretty. Stepping to the side to let them pass, we exchanged smiles and words about what a lovely afternoon.

I continued toward my car and thought about the couple. I couldn't remember whether they were holding hands, but it *seemed* like they were, or soon would be.

Back at my house, I settled in to read a bit. Even thought about practicing the bass for a while but couldn't muster enough initiative to upright it from its usual dominant position, lying on its side in the middle of the living room floor—instead of in a perfectly functional stand in the corner. After a light dinner, I read some more and went to bed. I wasn't really sleepy, but I wanted to do what I could to bring Monday on. With luck, Karen Settle would know something that would lead us to Trigger's killer.

Monday morning, I called Elly at work. I keep those calls to her at work short. She said she knew I looked forward to having lunch at the Dunes and talking with Karen Settle. I said, "I hope she will actually talk."

Elly said, "I have faith in you Harrison, and your ability to get about anyone to talk."

"Yeah, right," I said.

"It's true," she said, and I could tell she was smiling.

I waited until almost one o'clock before I left my house to drive down to Nags Head and the Dunes restaurant near Whalebone Junction. Pulling into the spacious parking lot, I took a spot off near the side of the restaurant. I sat there a moment or two. *Okay, be charming and non-threatening, Harrison, and let her know she can trust you.*

I got out of the car and went in.

The lunch crowd was definitely winding down. A smiling hostess asked me if I wanted a booth, but I saw Karen Settle off near the counter to the left, a more casual area. "There'd be fine," I said, indicating the tall tables and bar stools near where Karen stood. Karen eyed me as the hostess led me to one of the tall tables. I perched on the bar stool at the table. Sun came in through windows on that side. I pretended to study the menu the hostess had left for me. From the corner of my eye, I saw Karen approaching.

She held an order pad in one hand. "Hello," she said. "What can I get you to drink?" Her voice sounded weak, hesitant, tense. She flexed her shoulders, trying to make them relax.

I looked at her and smiled, trying to make the smile as genuine as I could. And it was genuine. "Oh, water'll be fine for right now," I said. "May get coffee later."

"I'll get it," she said. "Give you time to decide from the menu." She was an experienced server, I knew, but her mannerisms today were those of a first-day-at-work youngster.

When she returned with the water—a tall glass, with ice, and a wedge of lemon on the lip—a few drops of water spilled on the table as she set it down.

"Sorry," she said quietly.

"That's no problem, Karen," I said, and dabbed at the water with my napkin before she could try to wipe it away.

She retrieved her order pad with a pen from a side pocket of the baggy cargo-style shorts she wore. Her hands trembled slightly, and she took a breath and moved her elbows in close to her body. That controlled her hands, almost. She looked questioningly at me. "Have you had time to . . ."

"Yes, Karen. The crab cakes are always good. Luncheon. That's what I'll have."

She didn't bother to write the selection down. A slight pause, and I took advantage of it. Softly, I said, "I hope we'll have a chance to chat a bit when you're not too busy."

She gave a shaky affirmative nod of her head, and said, "I'll put your order in."

Only one other couple, probably in their late twenties, occupied a nearby tall table, and they appeared to be winding up their lunch. The young woman laughed at something her companion said, and then took a sip of her iced tea, which was nearly empty.

The luncheon plate came with two crab cakes and rémoulade sauce. French fries. A dab of coleslaw. The crab cakes were good, meaty, with lots of crab and not that much filling. I was hungrier than I thought I would be. But I made myself eat slowly, keeping a furtive eye on the diminishing luncheon crowd.

Karen Settle was not all that busy, yet she kept active with busywork, glancing in my direction every so often. In a few minutes she came back to my table and said, "Everything okay?"

"Excellent," I said. Then even more quietly, I said, "Can we talk soon?"

She looked distressed and didn't answer right away. I didn't like the hesitation.

"Soon?" I repeated.

That shaky affirmative nod of her head again. "Yes, soon." Her voice was almost a whisper. She scurried away.

The young couple at the other tall table had left. I was the only diner in that section of the restaurant. The hostess exchanged pleasantries with two businessmen who had had a late lunch.

Karen Settle stood with her back near the counter. She

glanced around and took a deep breath before approaching my table. I almost felt sorry for her. She was burdened with something she needed to rid herself of, yet she was obviously in real mental and emotional turmoil about it.

She carried an empty tray to clear my table. She kept her head down, not meeting my eyes. Resting the tray on the edge of the table, she muttered, "I don't want to be involved. Please. I don't want to be involved."

"You won't be. I promise you. You have my word on it. You won't be involved." I smiled at her, partly to try to reassure her and partly for appearances in case the hostess or anyone else might see us talking. I wanted it to appear to be a casual, friendly conversation.

Karen put my mostly empty plate on the tray, taking her time. "I was sick that day . . . and had to leave work early. I'm never sick. But I was that day, and throwing up and everything." She rushed her words together, wanting to get through with it.

She gathered my flatware, almost dropping the knife, and put it on the tray. The flatware made a clanking sound that was loud in the quietness that surrounded us.

"I knew I couldn't drive all the way home—I live down on Hatteras." Like most natives, she pronounced it Hat'rus.

"I understand," I said.

"So I went straight to Trigger's. And went right in. Didn't knock or anything." She glanced around and busied herself a bit more with appearing to clear the table. A slight embarrassment edged through. "I was in a hurry to get to the bathroom."

She did that thing with her shoulders again.

"I didn't pay any attention to the fact that Trigger's car was there, and another car, too. I was in a hurry." That embarrassed half-smile. "I wasn't sure I could make it. To the bathroom."

"I know the feeling," I said. And I waited.

"Had to go right past Trigger's bedroom." She took a

breath and leveled her eyes at me. "They were in there. They were, you know, doing it . . . or getting ready to do it . . . or just finishing maybe." She couldn't hold her eyes on mine. "Trigger saw me, but I don't think he did." She nodded. "I don't think he did. And nobody knows about him."

"When was this, Karen?" I asked.

"Two days before she was . . . before that terrible thing happened to her."

Now the real question: "Who was it, Karen? Who was the person there with Trigger?"

Very softly, she pleaded, "I can't get involved. Please. I don't want to . . ."

"I promise you."

Her hands trembled as she picked up my water glass. She wiped one hand with the cloth she had brought. "It was . . . it was Mr. Schweikert. Mr. Rick Schweikert."

Chapter Thirteen

I did my best. I really did. Trying to keep my face neutral, not let the shock explode my features. *Jesus Christ. Mr. Holier-than-thou himself. Schweikert, doing a little Afternoon Delight with a soon-to-be rape and murder victim.*

"Don't get me involved. Please don't," she continued to plead in a hoarse whisper. "He sort of scares me. I mean the district attorney and everything."

"Former district attorney," I said.

The hostess watched us. A faint expression of concern touching her eyes and brow. So I got a big grin and said, "The crab cakes were the very best I've had in a long time."

For the barest second, Karen looked puzzled. "Oh . . . I'm glad you enjoyed." She gave me the check.

Still maintaining a forced smile, I said more quietly, "I've promised you. No involvement. Don't worry."

I sidled down off the tall stool.

Since the hostess maintained a sideways glance toward us, Karen said rather loudly, pasting a smile on her lips, "Come back to see us."

"Most definitely," I said loudly.

Then, I turned back to Karen, and in a more conversational tone, I said, "Did you make it in time?"

"Huh?"

"The bathroom. Did you make it in time?"

Then it registered on her. A blush, but it didn't diminish the big, genuine smile—the first that day—that lit up her face. "Yes . . . yes, but . . . just barely."

Grinning, I waved a goodbye.

Outside, though, that grin faded right away. I sat in my car without starting the engine. Jeez, but I wrestled with the image of Schweikert there with Trigger. In some way, it was difficult to imagine; while in another, it seemed to fit right into the secret personality I suspected he had all along.

There was that obsession he had with his shirts, making sure they were ironed perfectly. The microscopic blue cotton under Trigger's fingernail. The blue cotton shirts Schweikert favored. So neatly done. Would that neatness trait of his translate to the folded placement of the victim's clothes? *Don't start building too many angles, Harrison. Take it slow.* What should I do first? Talk to Balls and Odell, that's for sure. At the same time protect Karen Settle as promised. I could do that, and I would do that.

Starting the engine, I pulled slowly out of the parking area to the edge of the highway. After waiting for a break in the traffic, I made my left into the center lane and waited for the traffic behind me, then eased forward—toward Manteo and the courthouse.

I drove more slowly than usual, my mind still whirling about. It was as if my thinking sapped the forward thrust of my vehicle. I sped up a bit when I realized a couple of cars were crowding behind me on the main road in Manteo. Turning at Budleigh Street. I found a parking space near the restricted parking beside the courthouse.

After parking, I started walking toward the rear of the courthouse. Balls' Thunderbird was parked at the head of the restricted area. Good. That meant he was probably around here, and hopefully with Odell upstairs—unless they were both off somewhere in the county making America safe for us citizens.

A deputy came out the back side door as I approached; I recognized him. and he apparently knew me, for he said, "Agent Twiddy's upstairs with Odell Wright."

"Thanks . . ." I checked his silver nametag, ". . . Deputy

Duval."

At the top of the stairs, I heard the sheriff tell Balls and Odell he appreciated the update. They were apparently just leaving the sheriff's office. When they saw me, Odell nodded pleasantly and Balls said, "Gawd, talk about a bad penny always showing up . . ." But he couldn't hide a trace of a smile. Balls being Balls.

"Yes, good to see you, too, Balls." I grinned at Odell and shook my head.

Odell said, "Tell us you've got some news . . . because we sure don't have anything."

I followed them into Odell's office.

"Well, we do got something," Balls said. "What we got is a lot of stuff that don't work, don't lead us anywhere."

I sat quietly for a moment, forming how I wanted to say what I had to say. I started to speak; but I got up and pulled the door shut and sat back down. They both eyed me.

Softly and speaking slowly, I said, "Two days before Trigger was killed, she had a visitor in the afternoon who no one apparently knew she was seeing. And she and this visitor were having sex, or getting ready for sex, or had just finished."

I took a breath.

Balls leaned his head to one side, looking hard at me, "And . . ."

"This person was Schweikert, Rick Schweikert," I said.

Balls leaned back in his chair, but kept his eyes trained on me. There was no fun in his face. All business. Dead serious.

Odell made some sort of sound, like an intake of breath, or a gasp or something.

Balls' glare was intense. "That's a heavy statement you're making."

"I know it is," I said. I met his eyes; I didn't waiver.

"Wanna tell me—tell us—how you know this?" Balls said.

"I can't," I said. "I promised not to get—not to get that person—involved in any way."

"Christ, Weav, that's awfully damn serious. I mean . . ."

"Yes, I know it is."

"And I know you don't like him, but . . ."

"This has nothing to do with not liking him. I was as surprised as you are. It's accurate. I'm convinced of that."

For the first time, Odell spoke up. "Actually, it fits in with what Snyder, that ex-boyfriend of Ms. Massey's, was saying. That he thought she was seeing somebody else that no one knew about . . . that she was keeping it real secret."

Balls made that "humpf" sound he makes sometimes. He shifted in his chair, took his eyes off me, and studied his hands pressed together in his lap. His fingers wrapped together.

He looked at Odell. "Looks like we're gonna have to have us a little chat with Mr. Schweikert." Then he turned back to me, glaring hard. "Don't want you anywhere around when we talk to him. Not even nearby. I want you gone. Vanished."

"I understand," I said. "I understand completely." With the animosity between Schweikert and myself, my presence would skew any objectivity that might come from their interrogation.

Head lowered like a big old bull, he kept those cop eyes on me. "And you damn well better be right about this."

"I am," I said. My voice was steady, and I stared right back.

Then the three of us were quiet. Very quiet. Except I think Odell muttered a half-moan to himself. "Oh, boy . . ." I knew how he must have felt, interrogating Schweikert, the former district attorney, who'd been an authority figure when Odell was still getting broken in as a young deputy with Dare County.

I sat up straighter in my chair, shoulders back. "True, I don't care for Schweikert. I don't like him. I think he's a pompous ass. But . . ."

Balls used that pause to interject, "But . . . what?"

"I can't see him as . . . as a rapist . . . killer." Leaning forward, I said, "If he's already having sex with her, then why . . . I know, I know, sex can go wrong. But the other thing . . ." My words were tumbling together more than I liked, so I tried to slow down. "The other thing, if our theory . . ." I saw the look Balls gave me when I used the phrase "our theory." I changed to, "If *your* theory is correct, and this is the work of a serial rapist, I have even a harder time seeing Schweikert in that role."

"So do I," Odell said in a subdued voice. "Even more trouble seeing him as a serial killer."

Balls shook his head. "You both know, same as I do, that a serial killer can be the person least suspected. The guy, who in every other aspect of his life, is normal. Leads a normal life. Maybe married. Have a family. Whole Jack Armstrong shit." He stopped. "Except . . ."

"You're right, of course," Odell said.

Again, it was so quiet I could hear the ticking of the clock the familiar mutterings of indistinct voices in the hall or from other offices.

Balls was the next to speak. He looked at Odell. "When?"

Odell obviously understood the question. He shook his head. "Not this afternoon." He glanced up at the clock. "He usually comes around here at the courthouse most every morning, late. Maybe we could catch him then."

I know that appealed as less confrontational to Odell. His unease at the task of interrogating Schweikert was palpable.

"That'll work," Balls said. He rolled his shoulders and began hiking his big body up from the chair, pressing the palms of both hands into the small of his back as he stood. "Meantime, I'm going to hell home."

He turned to me. I had stood also. "And you keep your damn mouth shut."

I gave a quick and energetic nod of my head. "You better believe it," I said.

"We all will," Balls added.

Odell remained seated behind his desk.

Balls put a big paw on the doorknob but didn't turn it yet. "I'll be back in the morning—right after this dirty-neck newspaper guy buys me one of those three-egg omelets at Henry's."

I managed a grin. "What time?"

"Meet me there at seven-thirty."

"See you then," I said.

"After we eat, you go on about your business, which ain't involved in any way with the courthouse. Go practice your cello."

"It's a bass fiddle."

"Whatever."

Balls left, and I was close behind him. I wanted to go downstairs and see Elly. She had to be wondering how it had gone with Karen Settle today. In the hall, Mabel had just finished saying something to Balls, who was headed down the back stairs.

Mabel turned to me. I smiled and spoke to her. She approached, shifting her weight from side to side. I was conscious of her ankles, and I know she was.

She said, "There's going to be a memorial service for Trigger on Saturday morning. Put on by a couple of the restaurant owners where she worked. Ten o'clock at the Methodist Church." She named which Methodist church. "A celebration of life, they call it."

"I'll be there," I said. I was sure, too, that a lot of people would be there also—friends, plus those who were morbidly curious about this latest rape and murder.

I thanked Mabel and headed for the front stairs. As I came down the stairs, I could see Elly in her office, writing something in a ledger. She looked up at me as I approached.

"Well," she said. "I wondered what had happened to

you."

"After lunch I came up the back way to talk with Odell and Agent Twiddy."

"I figured." She glanced over at co-worker Becky, who had a big, knowing smile on her face. She loved teasing Elly about her "someone special."

Elly studied my face. "You heading home?"

"Yes."

"Let's step outside a minute. On the porch." To Becky she said, "I'll be just outside. Right back."

"Sure," Becky said, still grinning.

Raising the panel in the counter, Elly joined me near the front door. She squeezed my hand, and I held the door open for her. We stepped out on the porch of the courthouse. The sun had moved lower in the west but was still bright and the air was fresh and warm.

"How did it go?" she asked.

"She talked," I said. "She was nervous, but she talked, and I promised not to get her involved. And I'm not . . . not going to get her involved."

"Did she tell you?"

"Yes." Then I gave a streamlined version of what Karen had said, how it all came about—and who the person was.

Elly nodded her head. She didn't seem all that surprised. Not like I was.

"You're not shocked?"

"No. Not as much as you might think."

I was puzzled. She saw it in my face.

"I'll tell you why . . . later." She gave my hand another tight squeeze. "Right now, I'd better get back inside."

"We'll talk," I said.

"Yes," she said. "Later."

Chapter Fourteen

Yes, I was puzzled as to why Elly didn't seem more surprised to hear about Schweikert. I know that women sometimes pick up on vibes from a guy that go right over some men's heads. Maybe she'd sensed that Schweikert was on the prowl. Maybe the son-of-a-bitch had tried to come on to Elly. Bastard better keep away from her.

I headed around the corner of the courthouse to Budleigh Street and my car. As I put my hand on the door, I remembered the home bills of Trigger's that I wanted to see. For a moment, I thought about going back upstairs to mention that to Odell. Thought better of it and sat in my car and called Odell on my cell phone.

I explained about the home repair bills that I wanted to see—on the off-chance there might be link between the Ferguson woman and Trigger. A really off-chance, I acknowledged.

Odell agreed with that, the off-chance bit. But he said, "Worth a shot, anyway." Then he added, "Yes, Deputy J.R. Phillips said you came by last Friday, I think it was. She said she wasn't sure what you wanted."

"That was it," I said.

"Okay, but not tomorrow," Odell said. "I think we may be busy talking to someone and Agent Twiddy doesn't want you around. I agree. Best not to be."

"Absolutely," I said.

"I'll get a folder with Ms. Massey's records. Credit card printouts, receipts. She had good records, and anything we may have on the Ferguson case. That won't be much." I sensed he was making a note to himself. "Day after tomorrow? Wednesday?"

"Sounds good," I said.

"If it looks like earlier, I'll let you know."

That evening, after a light supper and before time for Elly to be getting Martin ready for bed, I gave her a ring. After a bit of preliminary chit-chat, I got to what I was most curious about—her apparent lack of surprise that Schweikert was the mystery afternoon lover of Trigger's.

She said, "I don't think Trigger was the first one for Mr. Schweikert. I think he'd been . . . been trolling about for some time."

"You picked up on that, huh?" I said. "I guess women can pick up on things that men miss."

"Yes," Elly said, "and vice-versa. You men pick up on some things that we women miss."

"True." I was quiet a beat or two. Then, I had to ask, "Did that bastard try to come on to you?"

Elly gave a little chuckle. "Oh, so that's it. Are you a little jealous?"

"Well, yes, I would be if . . ."

"Don't worry, Harrison. But I am flattered that you'd be jealous."

"Of course I would."

"Years ago, when I first moved back here and started work at the courthouse, he tried to . . . to make overtures. But he didn't get anywhere. Number one, he's married, and number two, he is not at all appealing as far as I'm concerned. Maybe so to some women, but certainly not to me." I could tell she was smiling. "So you have nothing to worry about, Mr. Crime Writer."

I was a little embarrassed, I guess, and vaguely ashamed for having queried. But, hell, I'm only human. "Thank you, Elly. You're my sweetheart. You know that," I said.

We talked a bit longer and I could hear Martin in the background wanting his mother's attention, so we said goodnight.

I sat there by the phone for a few minutes. Maybe we ought to go ahead and get married. It was almost certain to happen one of these days. I guess it was understandable that both of us were skittish, afraid of the hurt that had come with the deaths of our spouses.

The next morning, shortly before seven-thirty, I was at Henry's awaiting Balls' arrival. I stood on the front porch. The sun was bright and the sky was blue. I gazed eastward, out toward the ocean—across the Bypass and the Beach Road—and not visible at all from where I stood, but I could still imagine it. Very real to me.

I smiled at a number of customers who came, one after the other. A steady flow of the breakfast crowd.

Right at seven-thirty, Balls pulled up in his vintage Thunderbird and parked well back to the rear, as far as possible from other cars. As always, he parked nose out in case he had to make a quick run.

He approached me, head down. I had a big smile all ready. Expecting his usual banter. There was no banter. He nodded a solemn greeting.

We didn't step inside immediately. "What's the matter, Balls?"

"Oh, nothing. What makes you think something's the matter?"

"Bullshit, Balls. You know better than try to bullshit an ol' bullshitter."

"Yeah," he said, hands in his trouser pockets. This pushed back the folds of his rumpled lightweight cotton sports coat. His holstered sidearm was visible. Usually, he would have stashed it under his front seat to come into a restaurant. He surveyed the horizon, then looked back at me.

"Lorraine's getting real depressed again." He spoke of his wife of many, many years. "She was up this morning, early, sitting in the living room on the sofa. Just sitting there. But I could tell she'd been crying." He was silent as two businessmen came past us to enter the restaurant.

Softly, I said, "I'm sorry, Balls."

"Yeah . . . well . . . She says she gets lonesome with the children gone . . . and me working all the time. But I don't know. Maybe it's something else." He shook his head. "Naw, that's a lot of it. Me working all the time. Not spending time with her. You know, doin' things. We don't just do things. She's right about that."

Three more customers smiled at us and said it was a lovely day as they went into the restaurant.

"Guess we better go inside," Balls said. He tried a grin. "'Fore these bastards eat all the food."

I held open the door for him and we went inside. I spoke to Linda, who along with her husband Henry, own the place. She is pretty and I always tell her that she looks pretty, for she does, and her hair, which has been prematurely gray for some years, is one of her crowning glories.

We were guided to a booth about halfway down. Balls slid in first, facing the front so he could see anyone entering or leaving. He also took a quick look around at the other diners. Always alert, and not seeming to be. We were given menus. I glanced at mine. Balls didn't bother. "I know what I want," he said.

Then, with a tilt of his head toward Linda at the front. "No wonder women like you. You're always telling 'em how pretty they are."

"I don't tell *all* women that, Balls."

"Enough of 'em."

"I like women," I said.

He shrugged. "No fooling."

"I don't mean women, women. I mean women, people."

He gave me a look. "I don't know what'n hell you're talking about."

"Not just as female . . . but as people." I grinned at him.

"I guess I'm a feminist."

He dismissed me with, "Whatever."

The waitress approached. I had seen her before over the years. She took food orders solemnly and brooked no crap from any of the customers.

I ordered the three-egg omelet, ham and American cheese, whole-wheat toast, coffee, water.

Balls said, "I'll take the three-egg omelet, with ham, bacon, crabmeat, red peppers, cheese, a side order of hash-brown potatoes, double order of white-bread toast, and a tall glass of tomato juice with crushed ice. Oh, and a side order of country ham, not overcooked." He paused and looked at her.

She had made one quick note on her order pad. She looked right back at him. "No mushrooms?"

"Huh?"

"No mushrooms on your omelet? You got about everything else."

I detected the slightest trace of a well-concealed smile playing around her eyes and lips.

"Didn't I say mushrooms?"

"No, you didn't. I figured you didn't want to overburden the cook."

"Well, heck, let's add mushrooms, too. Cook can rest later."

She turned and left. I definitely caught what was almost a smile.

Waiting for our food, we were silent for only a moment or two before I said, "Sorry that Lorraine is having one of those . . . those periods of depression. She's had them before, hasn't she?"

"Yeah. Been a while. And she usually snaps out of them. I don't know . . . seems like this one is tied into, like I said, you know, my work and her being alone a lot." He looked at me and I had the impression he could see the pain of memory in my face.

"Nothing like what you went through," he said. "I mean it depresses me that she's depressed, but . . . what you went through. Not like that."

He referred to Keely, my late wife. She had been a wonderfully talented jazz singer. Could really have been big time. But depression became more and more frequent. Deep, deep depression where no one could reach her. I tried, and we had professional help for a while. Nothing helped. There were pills, and that's what she finally did it with. I came home that afternoon. She lay in the bed on her side with her back to me. I touched her, and it was like touching a statue.

It took me months—years, if I admit it—to get over her suicide, to accept that there was nothing I or anyone else could do. Dwelling on it in the beginning, especially, I had become almost a basket case myself.

Our waitress came with the food on a large round tray. She put mine down, and then Balls' omelet. His omelet bulged at the sides. She had his tall glass of tomato juice with crushed ice and a separate plate for his double order of toast. He looked at his toast. She could tell he was about to ask for jelly. She pointed to the container of assorted packets of jelly there on the table.

Balls said, "Thanks."

She stood there a second longer. "The cook's gonna take a break now," she said, and she actually gave a half-smile at Balls. She nodded and left. I was glad she didn't ruin her image by saying something like the all-too-usual, "You guys enjoy."

We dug right in.

But with a mouthful of food, Balls said, "I guess I could retire." He swallowed, with the help of a slug of his tomato juice, crunching some of the ice. "But what would I do? Get a private investigator's license? Try to catch cheating husbands or wives? Deadbeat dads?" He shook his head and went back to his omelet and toast, then a bite of the country ham. It wasn't overcooked.

Eating mostly in silence, it was a couple of minutes before I brought up the basic topic of the day. "How do you feel about talking with Schweikert today?"

"Who says I'm gonna talk to Schweikert?"

"Aw, Balls, you know you are."

He shoveled in more food. "Aw, it'll go all right. Try to make it as casual as possible. He ain't gonna like that we know about him getting a little on the side."

"A suspect in your mind?"

"Everybody's a suspect."

"That's a lot of crap, Balls. You don't believe that."

He opened the third packet of jelly, scooped it out onto a triangle of toast. "To a certain extent I do. But Schweikert? I don't know." He puffed out a breath of air. "I'm not crazy about him either, but I hope he's got a great alibi—like an all-night meeting with the Kiwanis Club or something."

I waited a beat or two before speaking. "As I said, I could—with a stretch—see him as a suspect in one rape." I shook my head. "But a serial rapist? Murderer? I have a harder time."

The waitress came back. She surveyed our plates. "Anything else?"

"No thank you," I said. "It was good, as always. Take a check when you can."

She produced the check and put it face down on the table between us. I took it. She said to Balls, "I didn't charge you for the mushrooms. But wanted you to have them . . . and not go away hungry." There was definitely a smile this time.

Balls got that big grin of his. "This should hold me until almost lunchtime," he said.

Outside, I walked with Balls back to his Thunderbird. We stood there a moment; he watched my face. "You're sure about the sex thing—Trigger and Schweikert."

"Absolutely," I said. "The person who told me witnessed it." It wouldn't hurt to say a little bit more. "And I believe her. She is frightened about knowing it."

"Maybe . . . just maybe . . . she's got reason to be frightened." He opened the door to his car and got ready to leave.

I walked on to my car, head down. I did raise one hand as sort of a wave goodbye as I heard the rumble of Balls' Thunderbird pull out of the parking area.

Chapter Fifteen

I wished I could be there today when Balls and Odell had their little sit down come-to-Jesus chat with Schweikert. No way, of course. Afterward, though, I'd manage to get a fill in from Odell or Balls. I was convinced of that.

Meanwhile, I'd do my best to put that out of my mind. I still wanted to get to the courthouse and go through those household bills and receipts of Trigger's, compare them with what little I knew about business services the Ferguson woman may have used.

Best I stay away from the courthouse all day today, but I could surely go back there tomorrow.

I spent the rest of the day and into the afternoon catching up on email and other correspondence. Paying a few bills. That sort of thing. I tried, mostly unsuccessfully, not to think about the Trigger and Ferguson rape/murders. That evening I did start a list of things I knew concerning each of the cases, starting with any similarities, like the neatly folded clothes and the absence of panties.

Then I admonished myself. This wasn't my case.

Face it, you can't help it. You are obsessed with trying to solve puzzles like this one. True.

The next morning, after dawdling an inordinate amount of time sipping coffee and sitting out on the deck, I gave in to myself and decided to head for Manteo and the courthouse . . . after I'd enjoyed a long shower and took my time getting dressed.

At almost eleven, I called Elly to see whether she might have lunch with me. I was pleased that she said she'd be happy to. Told her I'd be there close to noon.

As I drove, I noticed that a few clouds had started building in the southwest. Something I've come to realize about anyone who lives at the Outer Banks, or who spends a lot of time here, is that they have a constant and ongoing interest in the weather. Almost anyone can tell you what the latest weather forecast is, when the next rain will be coming, or wind, or coastal flooding, or whether we need be worried about the low-pressure area lurching about in the Atlantic.

In Manteo, I parked off Sir Walter Raleigh Street in the unpaved alleyway next to the coffee shop. Squeezed into a space that was one in from the sidewalk. I made sure there was enough room between my car and the next so that no one would be dinging the other when opening doors.

Stepping into the Register of Deeds' office, I didn't see Elly. But Becky, after greeting me, turned her head toward the little office off to the side and said, "Elly, Someone Special is here to see you."

A moment later, Elly came out of the inner office, a nice smile lighting her face. "Are you Someone Special?"

"Hope so," I said. "Want to go eat?" Then I added, even though I knew she would have to decline "Becky, want to join us?"

She raised one shoulder and made a mock grimace. "Thanks, but someone's gotta stay here and watch the office while you two are off snuggling in a booth somewhere."

With a phony look of stern disapproval, Elly said, "We'll probably be *snuggling* at one of the tables at Ortega'z."

The restaurant, featuring Mexican and Southwestern fare, was a few doors down from the courthouse, and we got a table near the front. A young man, who gave his name as Phil, said he would be our server and asked what we cared to drink. Elly wanted sweetened iced tea and I opted for water, no lemon. Casually, we perused the menus, and settled on chicken tacos, which we had had before. They were always good.

As soon as Phil had brought our drinks and I'd placed our orders for the tacos, Elly looked at me and spoke softly. "Mabel told me this morning that yesterday Deputy Wright and Agent Twiddy had a long 'talk' with Rick Schweikert." She used a finger of each hand to put quote marks around "talk."

True to form, Mabel served as a conduit of information about what was going on—and to whom it should be relayed. Mabel didn't broadcast information. She was selective who was targeted. She was fully aware of my interest in the case, and she knew that by telling Elly, I would get the word.

"Do you know how it went?" I asked.

"No. Mabel didn't volunteer any more than that." Elly stopped speaking as Phil arrived with our food.

"Enjoy," he said.

Casting a tilt of her head toward the heaping chicken tacos, with extra salsa and sour cream on the side, Elly said, "That was certainly quick." Then, "Mabel did say the three of them were in Odell's office for forty minutes or more."

I doctored my taco with a bit more sour cream and salsa, and took an appreciative taste. "Good," I said.

With that slight cock of her head, Elly said, "'Good' as in taco, or 'good' as in that they spent a long time with Schweikert?"

"Both, I guess." A moment or two later, I said, "I'll get a briefing from Balls or Odell."

"They wouldn't tell him where they got the information, would they?"

"They don't know," I said. "I didn't tell them where I got the information."

She gave a short, mirthless chuckle; then swallowed the bite she had taken, took a sip of her iced tea. "They know they got the information from you."

"Yes, but I was only the messenger . . . and I don't think they would have mentioned me in any way. Knowing how Schweikert feels about me, that would have derailed the . . .

the topic, and get Schweikert off on how I was trying to ruin him, or some such tack."

We ate in silence for a couple of minutes before Elly, holding her fork in her right hand and absently touching the edge of her taco shell lightly with the tines, looked up at me and said, "What do you think, Harrison? Do you think Schweikert could or would do something . . . like something that was done?"

She leaned back in her chair but kept her eyes on me. She said, "I know you don't like him, but I also know, Harrison, knowing you, you wouldn't let that dislike be a deciding factor in what you really think and believe. Not in something like this."

"Thank you for a vote of confidence or whatever it was." I tried a grin, and maybe succeeded. "The short answer is no. No, I don't think he is a real suspect in these two rapes and murders."

I could tell she weighed how I had phrased my response. "You're obviously linking both cases together. I've thought about that. But seems like no one wants to talk about that possibility . . . at least not openly."

"Yes, there's some indication the two are linked," I said.

"Aw, come on, Harrison. This is me you're talking to. Don't try to fuzz around with half-answers."

I did grin this time. "Okay. You're right. As much as you've been through with me, you deserve more than vague cop-talk. Yes, Odell, and I think Balls too, believe that this is the work of a serial rapist/murderer. I can't see Schweikert in that role—much as I dislike him." I took breath. "But that doesn't mean that he couldn't have . . ."

"I know, I know. 'We can't rule out anyone.'"

"True."

Phil came to our table. "Care for anything else? We've got some great desserts."

"Thanks, but no thanks. It was very good. Check when you get a chance," I said. When he left, presumably to get our check, I said to Elly, "I should have asked you about dessert, but . . ."

"Heavens no," she said. "I couldn't quite finish the taco."

She had done a hearty job on it, though. She always had a great appetite, and I could not understand why she never seemed to gain an ounce.

After I had settled the bill and tip, we strolled back to the courthouse. "I'll go inside with you," I said, "and then wander upstairs, maybe catch Odell. Don't know whether Balls came here today or not."

She looked up at me as we walked slowly to the front of the courthouse. A smile brushed her lips. "I've haven't heard Agent Twiddy. And usually when he's in the courthouse, even upstairs, you can hear him from time to time."

"Yes, a deep rumble," I said, "just like his beloved car."

I told Elly I'd see her later, and I went upstairs.

The interrogation room was empty and Odell's office door was ajar. He was on the phone. He saw me, and still talking, invited me in with a scooping motion of one hand.

Entering quietly, I took one of the seats in front of his desk. He wound up his phone conversation with, "If you think of anything else, I'd appreciate a call—at any time. You've got both of my numbers." He put the phone down, gave a short shake of his head. To me, he said, "Anything new with you?"

"I was hoping maybe you'd cracked the case—cases—by now."

"Nothing. Nothing."

Being guardedly discreet, I eased out of the chair enough to push the door shut and settled back in the chair. Keeping my voice low, I said, "How did it go with Mr. Schweikert?"

Again, he shook his head and got what was probably an exaggerated expression of "you-wouldn't-believe-it" with his eyebrows and twist of his mouth. He said, "It was pretty damn emotional in the beginning. Balls and I both were talking with him, here in this office, with the door shut." He did that thing with his mouth. "He was loud enough, I expect Mabel or anyone else could have heard him in the beginning."

"He deny seeing Trigger?"

"In the beginning, yeah. But you know Balls. He can be sort of . . . sort of persistent. Keep on pushing. And, yes, after a while, Mr. Schweikert admitted seeing her, having sex . . . or being 'intimate' with her, as he put it."

I didn't say anything.

Odell stared at his hands, which stretched in front of him atop his desk. He kept moving his fingers in a silent drumbeat. "Tell you the truth, Weav, I began to feel kind of sorry for him. Here he was, the former DA, being interrogated by me, a deputy in the sheriff's office, and big ol' tough Agent Twiddy. It was a shitty place for him to be in—and not one he was used to, that's for sure."

I hesitated a moment. What Odell was saying made so much sense. And it told me even more about Odell, an excellent investigator and lawman . . . and at the same time an empathetic and feeling human being. Then I said, "A suspect? What do you think?"

He stopped the drumbeat with his fingers but kept staring at his hands, as if he willed his fingers to be still. His lips were compressed. "I know we can't rule out anyone—that's not true, 'cause we can rule out some persons—but I have a hard time seeing him as a real suspect." He flexed his shoulders. "Still, strictly between you and me, I'm not ruling him out completely. And neither has Balls, I don't think." Another pause, and then, "I wish he had a better alibi for where he was that night—besides just being home with his wife."

I kept my eyes on Odell. "If this is the work of a serial rapist . . ."

"Yeah, I know. It sounds like whatever he had going with Trigger was consensual."

"We both know, of course, that a serial killer can have consensual sex. He doesn't have to always be a rapist," I said.

"Yeah, Balls mentioned the same thing," Odell said.

"Balls? What does he think?" Before Odell could respond, I said, "And where is Balls today?"

Odell appeared somewhat distracted, as if he was thinking about the serial aspect of the case. Then he said, "Huh? Balls? He's working on something over near Hertford. A little bit closer to home for him. His wife is . . ."

"Yes, I know."

"Balls' opinion is about the same as mine . . . or mine is about the same as his. Either way."

Odell stared out the window. I don't think he was looking at anything. Only that thousand-yard stare.

It was time for me to leave Odell, let him concentrate on something other than my questions. "I'll get out of your hair, Odell. Let you get to it."

"Yeah," he said softly, but he wasn't focused on what I'd said.

I stood. "One thing, though. Did you get a chance to get those household bills and receipts of Trigger's together? And anything you might have from the Ferguson file. I'd really like to go through them."

This got Odell's attention, and he became more animated. "Sure, sure," he said, with even a touch of enthusiasm. "Heck, maybe you'll see something that could really be of help." He stood, also, and stretched out his back a bit. "Who knows what bits of information may get us off dead center?"

I did a hint of a grin, which was out of place in that I was blithely making light of something that, indeed, was not light nor should be treated that way. "I just hope there isn't another—another *happening*—that gets us off dead center."

"So do I," he said solemnly. "So do I."

Chapter Sixteen

Before I left, Odell said it would probably be tomorrow before he could get anything in the way of spending records for Francine Ferguson and Trigger Massey.

While I knew it would not take long to get both files, hand them to me, and let me go over them in the empty room next door to Odell, for some reason he wanted to put it off. Maybe he wanted to think about it further, whether he would be compromising any protocol by permitting me to study the records.

Perhaps he wanted to check with Balls. I don't think he would bring it up with the sheriff, who, I was sure, would nix the idea—if only because potentially it might in some way come back to bite them politically, or even legally in a trial. I could see the political aspect, but not the legal. Heck, here was a writer looking over spending records. What was wrong with that?

At any rate, I wasn't overly concerned about it. After all, it was one hell of a long shot, and probably wouldn't amount to anything anyway. Tomorrow, or the day after, or the day after that . . . no rush certainly. Unless there was another "happening."

When I got home, I checked on Janey, talked to her a bit. Yes, talked to a parakeet. She likes that. She showed her appreciation by chirping loudly and doing her head-bopping dance.

Turning to my work area or "office" on the dinette table, I consulted my calendar for the next day. I had almost forgotten. Tomorrow morning, I was scheduled for an early flying lesson with Sam—Samantha Inez Davis—and then to-morrow night Jim Watson wanted us to get together for a re-hearsal with a new trombone player. Jim led the little jazz group that I played bass with. Busy times. And I wanted to be able to get back to work on the book I was writing; it had been pushed back by current projects from my editor, not to mention my unofficial involvement in a murder investiga-tion. Two rape/murder investigations, matter of fact.

After a light supper, I started to catch up on the *PBS News Hour*, when Elly called. I quickly muted the television and answered the phone.

Elly said, "I just got off the phone with Karen Settle. She called, all upset because she was convinced you had told the authorities that she was the one who said that Mr. Schweikert was having an affair with Trigger. I tried to tell her . . ."

"You know I didn't reveal her identity," I said.

"I know you didn't. But she said Mr. Schweikert came into the Dunes at lunch today—something he never does—and kept staring at her, like he was mad, and it made her very nervous. So that she was scared."

"You have her number? Karen's number?"

"Yes. Her cell phone." She gave it to me.

"I'll call her. Assure her that she has been kept anony-mous."

"Good luck," Elly said. "Call me when you finish."

Karen's cell phone rang three times before she answered with a cautious, reluctant, "Hello . . ."

"Karen, this is Harrison Weaver, and I want you to know that your name, your identification, has never been re-vealed by me, as I promised you."

She didn't say anything, so I continued.

"When I talked with Chief Deputy Odell Wright and SBI Agent Twiddy, I told them what I knew about—about the fact that a certain person was having a relationship, or sex, with Trigger. They asked me, of course, how I knew that, and I told them that I had it from a very reliable person whose identity I could not reveal. And they did not push me on trying to get me to reveal how I knew it."

Karen's voice, layered with what may have been a touch of aggression or hostility, came across a little jerky, like she was taking shallow breaths. "Well, I think he found out some way. He came to the Dunes today and sat there a long time and kept staring at me. I didn't wait on him. Kim did. But he kept looking at me like he was mad, like he hated me, and it made me so nervous I dropped a big tray of dishes. I never do that."

"Karen, you've got to believe me. I promised you I would not reveal your name or your identity and I didn't. I keep my word, and I kept my word."

She said, "Somehow he knew—he had to—that the word was out and that I was involved somehow."

"Think about it, Karen. Trigger saw you that day. If she saw you, maybe he did too. Or Trigger told him. It probably didn't bother him in the beginning, but then yesterday *if* authorities talked with him about it, you know he got upset."

Of course, Odell and Balls had confronted him, but I didn't want to come right out and say that.

She was quiet another few seconds. Then she said, "I guess you're right. He probably knew I knew that same afternoon. But it didn't, you know, bug him until those lawmen started nosing around . . . and he thinks I'm the one who told on him."

Her voice rose a decibel or so. "And I had to be the one who told on him—Trigger couldn't. She was dead."

"Yes, but, Karen, you don't know, and the man we're talking about can't know for sure, who else Trigger might have told about her . . . her relationship."

"Maybe you're right," she said, "and I know you didn't give my name, but he did make me nervous today, and he scared me."

"You don't have anything to worry about, Karen. He's not going to do any more than he did today—and probably won't do that again. A onetime thing."

I hoped I was right.

Her voice was softer now. "Mr. Weaver, do you think he was the one who . . . who did that to Trigger?"

I tried to sound more upbeat than I felt. "No, Karen, no indeed. I don't think the lawmen do either. I think he has a good solid alibi as to where he was when that occurred."

Okay, I wasn't being all that honest. But it was the best thing to say.

As requested, I called Elly back and told her that I thought it went well with Karen Settle. After lingering with each other a couple of minutes, we said goodnight.

I was out at the Manteo airport before eight the next morning, Samantha, or Sam, waited for me in the lounge of the main building; she talked with the young man behind the counter. He perched on a high stool that swiveled, so he could easily get to the radios and other equipment behind the counter. While the airport is not a controlled facility, it is extremely active and there is a lot of radio chatter, even without air traffic control.

Sam is tall and athletic, with a great figure and strikingly handsome face, dominated by those high cheekbones. She has a longtime steady boyfriend, operator of a small but high-end construction company, who is as athletic as she is, and as physically attractive for a man as she is for a woman. Many a male pilot has looked longingly at Sam, lusting for her even more than they are for a brand-new Cessna aircraft. However, as the fates deal more often than not, they don't get either one.

"Morning, Sport," Sam said. "Ready to go punch through a few clouds?"

"Sure," I said. "But if this weather holds, as promised, we aren't going to see many clouds to punch."

She told the young man behind the counter that we

would be taking off soon. "Have fun," he said.

Sam and I strolled onto the back porch of the building and then headed to the right and a Cessna 172 parked on the edge of the tarmac.

As we got to the aircraft, Sam said, "This one has already been up for a short hop, and pre-flight checked. Just the same . . ."

"I know," I said. "You want me to do it thoroughly again."

"Absolutely. Want that ingrained in you."

I did the same routine as always, starting near the left door with the pitot tube and stall-horn indicator, fuel check, and worked my way around, ending with the engine's oil level, and running my hand over the propeller for any nicks or dings. Taking my place in the left seat, I tested the controls and double-checked gauges and instruments on the dash.

We buckled in good and wore headsets so we could talk clearly with each other.

"Fire her up," Sam said.

I cracked open my door a couple of inches and yelled, "Clear prop." That was another safety precaution Sam insisted on, even when we knew no one was close to the aircraft. The engine started immediately. My heart always beat faster with the feel of the engine vibrating our airframe. I kept the toe brakes engaged.

"You've checked the weather, the wind?" Sam said.

"Yes. Nine miles an hour from the southwest."

"Good." She grinned at me. "Out over the lovely Croatan Sound."

"Roger, that." I grinned back at her.

"Shit," she said, "sounding like a real pilot."

We taxied to the northeast end of the field, swung around, and got in position. Pressing hard with the toe brakes, I ran the rpm up on the engine and checked gauges again, including the magnetos.

Even though Manteo was not a controlled airport, as I said, Sam wanted me to get used to using the radio. I switched the toggle to talk to the young man behind the counter. "Cessna four-niner-zero set to takeoff."

"You're clear to go," came the radio response.

Sam nodded. With my left hand on the yoke and my right on the throttle, I advanced the thrust and eased my feet off the brakes, and we lurched forward and began our charge down the runway—always an exciting time. We picked up speed, then more speed, and then I felt us lifting off the runway and we were airborne, with the earth and then the sparkling waters of the sound slipping away beneath us.

I know I was smiling. I had to be.

Gaining altitude, I swung us to the right, heading over the northwest corner of Roanoke Island, with the town of Manteo down below off to the right.

Sam had me fly northwest toward the Wright Memorial Bridge and the pointy end of Currituck County. "Keeping Highway 158 as a reference point, get your altitude up to 750 and follow the highway toward Grandy," she said. "Make the same turns the highway does, and hold your altitude steady."

Good practice. More curves than you'd expect.

"Altitude," she alerted me a couple of times. But overall, I did well.

After a while we came back to Manteo and she had me practice one touch-and-go at the airport before I had to make my approach for a landing at the end of the lesson. We had to circle back once to give another pilot in a twin Piper time to take off. When he was clear. I did the base leg and came around to land.

As we got closer to touchdown, the airplane wanted to keep on flying. I did the landing, though, with a minimum of bounce. We taxied back to the main building and parked at the tarmac where we'd started. I shut down the engine and took a deep breath, looking over at Sam.

"Not bad, Sport. Not bad at all."

"Thanks." I know I grinned.

She unbuckled and did the same. "You know," she said, "it's probably past time for it, but I think you're ready to solo."

I stopped my grin. "Oh, I don't know, Sam . . ."

She started exiting the right side, paused, and said, "We'll see. Don't want you to worry about it, and I'll probably spring it on you when you're not expecting it, so you don't worry in advance."

I got out and folded the seatbelts neatly, closed the door. A solo flight was in the future, I always knew, but it did make me a little apprehensive thinking about it—and excited and proud at the same time. *Well, when it was right, and Sam, as cautious as she is, would use good judgment. So, I'm not going to think about it. Yeah, right.*

Inside, we penciled in a time for the next lesson. I was ready to leave when Sam, stepping aside with me and keeping her voice low, said, "I know you stay close to any investigations that are going on. What about the rapes and murders? The one earlier and the one just—what? last week?—of Trigger Massey?"

"They're still under active investigation. I don't know that anything . . ."

"My boyfriend is convinced it's a serial killer."

I started a dismissive hedge of some sort, but Sam continued.

"If it is a serial killer," she said, "then he thinks it's liable to happen again real soon."

"I certainly hope not," I said. Pretty lame, I know, but I didn't know what else to say.

I certainly didn't want to say what I really thought—that her boyfriend was probably right. There would be another one, and maybe sooner than we'd expected.

Chapter Seventeen

Upon leaving the airport, I mentally wrestled with the thought of swinging by the courthouse, checking on whether there was any progress on the investigation, and maybe stop in and speak briefly to Elly.

I was determined to be more in control and not give in to whims. Head back home, do my own work, and get ready late in the afternoon for a rehearsal with Jim Watson and the new trombone player.

If a break in either of the cases developed, I'd learn about it in short order, I was convinced.

However, so much for being in control of my whims. Unconsciously, I found myself swinging up Budleigh Street and parking near the front of the courthouse.

I went in the front door. At the Register of Deeds office, coworker Becky greeted me. "Elly had to go pick up Martin," she said. "The school called and said he had an upset stomach. Nothing serious, Elly said, and she'll probably be back after a while."

"Thanks," I said. "Ask her to give me a ring when she gets back. Want to make sure all is okay."

Stepping into the hall, I saw Deputy Dorsey coming down the stairs. "If you're looking for Chief Deputy Wright and Agent Twiddy, they've both left and said they wouldn't be back until later this afternoon."

Well, so much for that. I should have listened to my instincts to go straight home.

Then as I opened the front door to head back to my car, who comes slugging up the short steps but Schweikert.

He nodded a curt, "Weaver."

I nodded in return, and every bit as curtly: "Schweikert."

"Looking for more bodies, Weaver?"

"That's what I do best, Schweikert."

"Yeah, I've noticed."

Then, as if explaining something to a child, I said, "After all, I *am* a crime writer. That's what I write about—crime. And that frequently involves dead bodies."

"Yeah, they seem to follow you around."

What was all this on his part? A good defense is a good offense? Throw me off about his having had a sit-down with Balls and Odell? He had to know that as close as I was to both of them that they would have clued me in on their conversation with him.

Then I took my first real look at him. He appeared to be wearing yesterday's shirt. It was not as crisp and pristine as usual. Still much better than most of us looked, but not like his usual attire. And he had missed a small patch of whiskers under his left jaw line. Again, not like him. Maybe he was more worried about his situation and the confrontation with Balls and Odell, as civil as I'm sure that was, than he would want anyone to know.

He stepped close to me, his face inches from mine. I didn't move. Stood my ground. Stared right back.

"Well, you can quit looking for any bodies close to me, Weaver. There aren't any. So keep your nose away . . . or somebody could step on it."

Before I could respond—and I wasn't sure what I would have said—he wheeled and went quickly into the courthouse.

I stood there a moment. Dumbfounded. I replayed in my mind some snappy comebacks I could have blurted out. Something really snappy like, "Screw you." Yep, that'd be a worthy response from someone who is supposed to be literate. Too late now, anyway. As almost always, responses come to one after the opportune moment.

I walked slowly back to my car. All of the earlier exhilaration about a successful flying lesson and the thought of spending a happy moment or two with Elly had vanished.

Flopping into the driver's seat of my car, I took forever to turn on the ignition and head for home.

When I got home, the message light on my answering machine was blinking. It was a voice mail from Rose, my editor. And it was a solid compliment without her usual needling. She thanked me for the job I'd done on editing and rewriting the long exposé piece written—allegedly *written*—by that celebrity.

I really needed to get back to working on the book I was writing. I don't know. Seems I was having a difficult time settling down with it. I don't believe in writer's block: I do believe in writer's laziness and distraction caused by other interests, with maybe a fear of failure thrown in.

An element of distraction would come with the rehearsal tonight. Additionally, tomorrow night, I planned to attend our monthly writers' critique group. Actually, it was sort of an open mic—without the mic—and critique session combined. It was something of an obligation I felt we owed each other, the giving of support and encouragement to fellow ink-stained wretches. Writing can be a lonely and solitary endeavor, often accompanied by dampening feelings of inadequacy. Encouragement and support are needed.

This kind of over-extending myself happened from time to time, and was something I had to watch. That is, slowly, step by step, I would become involved in one thing after another until finally I felt overwhelmed, trapped, and unable to know which way to turn or which task should be tackled next—and ended up spinning my wheels.

Okay, Harrison, start ridding yourself of things. Too much going on. Get rid of some.

I forced myself to sit down, open the computer to the last pages of the novel in progress, reread those, make a couple of minor edits, and I was ready to begin writing again. In no time at all, I was back at it and moving along nicely.

Every now and then, Harrison, you got to take a stick and beat yourself with it, making your lazy self get with what you should be doing.

By late afternoon I was right proud of myself. I had written close to a thousand words, a sort of informal personal goal I set when writing. With computers, it's easy to do the word count. I've thought about earlier writers—Somerset Maugham, Trollope, Mark Twain, and even Hemingway—who had to do word count by hand. But they did it. Kept records of how much they were actually writing. As Hemingway reportedly said, "It's easy to hoodwink yourself."

Feeling I had earned the break, I got up from my workstation, stretched, and put the black canvas cover on my bass in preparation for tonight's rehearsal.

After a light supper, I headed toward Jim Watson's house at the south end of Kill Devil Hills. His place is on the sound side of the town rather than the ocean side.

Jim kept a stripped-down drum set Dane could use so he didn't have to bring his own for a rehearsal. Tell the truth, we had held very few rehearsals at Jim's. We were comfortable enough playing with each other and besides that, we had scores, or fake books, we could refer to when playing. A fake book, which years ago were illegal and had to be smuggled among musicians, is nothing more than a number of tunes with only the melody line written out and chord symbols appropriately placed. That's all that's needed.

When I got to Jim's, Dane was already there chatting with Jim. On piano, or keyboard, tonight was Frank Myers. We were lucky enough to have access to a couple of really good jazz piano players. They were hard to come by.

I thought Jim had said something about a *new* trombone player, but Tom Stevens, our regular, came sauntering in shortly after I arrived; his tall, loose-jointed frame appearing, as usual, that it might come unfastened at any moment, and an arm or a leg could fly out at some strange angle. With his friendly grin at everyone, he folded himself into a chair and started working on the slide of his horn, spraying water or oil, on it, and moving the slide up and down with his fingertips. His wrist was agile enough to produce a beautiful vibrato when needed. Frankly, though, I loved to hear him hit a note solid, and then meld into an exaggerated vibrato. That style always reminded me of the wonderful trombone solo featured on Stan Kenton's "The Peanut Vendor."

After we all got settled in and tuned up, it became obvious why Jim had called for this rehearsal. He looked a little embarrassed as he stood there, idly fingering the valves on his trumpet, the valves making an almost inaudible clicking sound. "I've really been working on trying to copy that opening run that Louis Armstrong does on 'West End Blues.' Ambitious, I know, and there's no way I can get it the way he did it, but I'll take a shot at it, and then—just like on the recording—the trombone slides in moaning, and we're off."

Jim looked at Frank and then me. "Doing it in B-flat . . . the Home Key . . . and standard 12-bar blues."

We nodded.

Jim stood, leaning a hip against the end of the piano, put his trumpet to his lips and played out that familiar intro. True, it might have been scaled down a bit from Armstrong's original, but it was damn good, and it made a shiver of appreciation tingle down my spine. And then Tom moaned in with his trombone, a wailing that carried us all into a slow blues.

When we finished, we all were enthusiastic and complimentary to Jim. "That was really great, Jim," I said. Frank stood up from the piano bench and shook Jim's free hand. "Well done, indeed, Satchmo," he said.

"Love the trombone, too," Dane said.

We did the blues number all the way through two more times, and then went to three other pieces that Jim wanted us to work on. Before we wound up, he announced that we had at least two afternoon gigs at Scarborough Faire in Duck starting early next month.

Back home, I trudged up the side stairs, cradling my bass awkwardly. I swear the bass gets heavier each year. Can't understand how it does that. Yeah, right.

I didn't bother taking the cover off the bass; laid it on its side in the middle of the living room. Do it later. I plopped down on the sofa.

Janey chirped away in her caged and then said, quite clearly, "Shit." And more chirping.

"I agree with you, Janey," I said.

After sitting there a few minutes, I eased up off the sofa, stepped over the neck of my bass fiddle, and checked the answering machine. There was one message. I sat on the little chair by the phone, and punched play. It was Odell.

He said, "I've finally gotten those household bills and receipts for you to look over when you want to. Got 'em here at my desk. Not much from the Ferguson file, but quite a few from Trigger Massey's records."

Well, tomorrow maybe I would get to it, although I really needed to stay here and work on that book; tomorrow night there was that open mic/critique group meeting. I agreed with Janey. Crap, there was too much I was getting myself involved with.

With a sigh, I got up and went to the kitchen, covered Janey's cage, and then went in the bathroom and washed my face and got ready for bed.

Chances were I'd feel better about things in the morning.

Chapter Eighteen

And it was true. I did wake up that morning feeling better. After a bite to eat and the usual coffee, I settled right down to work on the book, resisting the temptation to scurry to the courthouse. The book—and I was almost halfway through with it—centered on three high-profile unsolved murder cases in North Carolina. Coverage of the murders had gathered national attention. Rose was convinced this would be another good-selling book.

By mid-afternoon I took a break and called Elly. She was doing well and said it was unusually quiet at the courthouse. "Even Mabel doesn't have any news," she said with a chuckle.

I did speak briefly with Odell, and he confirmed, too, that nothing new had developed. He was frustrated by the lack of any leads. Balls was stymied as well, Odell said.

However, Odell did let slip that Balls was out on an interview, and that he might have something to report later.

I waited for Odell to say more. It was obvious after several seconds of silence that he was not saying more at this time. I wondered what Balls was up to. He was doing whatever he was doing by himself, without Odell. I knew I would find out eventually, but it did nag at me. Want to be in on the circle at all times. Can't help it.

At least I wasn't missing any of the inaction today, I figured, and I went back to work for another hour or more. Then it was time for a shower and to get ready for our monthly writers' meeting. I didn't have anything to read or ready to be shared, but I liked hearing others read and to learn what they were working on.

I was especially interested in hearing the latest writings of a new member of our group, Lila Quenton. Originally from Wisconsin, she had moved to the Outer Banks a year earlier and joined our group a couple of months ago. She was doing a long piece—part memoir, part fiction—about growing up with her bizarre and charmingly dysfunctional family in Wisconsin. Sections of the story were touching and sad and some so humorous they made a reader laugh aloud.

We met starting at six-thirty down in Nags Head at one of the art galleries. Free-lance journalist Kip Tabb headed the group and kept us going. He was working on at least two novels, and he was certainly another good writer.

While the number attending varied somewhat from month-to-month, there were eight of us there that night, which was fairly average. Lila read first, and discussed the progress in her story. She also gave an update on her total word count. I can't always estimate a person's age, but I pegged Lila as early thirties. She had almost shoulder-length reddish blonde hair and large blue eyes. As far as I could tell, she lived alone. One of the other writers said Lila moved here following a divorce. Like so many people, she had become familiar with the Outer Banks when her parents vacationed here years earlier.

During a break midway through the evening, I had an opportunity to chat with Lila and compliment her on her writing. While she had written quite a bit in college and shortly afterward, and had had a few short pieces published, this was the first real writing she had done in years. I wished her good luck on her writing and to keep it up.

We seemed comfortable with each other right from the start. I learned a bit more about her, and the fact that she was a regular runner and would be participating the coming weekend in a mini-marathon at the Outer Banks. Her day job involved something with one of the larger real estate firms here.

The meeting broke up close to nine. Some hung around a bit longer chatting. I said goodnight and went to my car and started the drive back home. It felt like a long day, and it was.

By midmorning the next day, I was surprised by a call from Balls. I hadn't heard anything from him for what seemed like forever—of course it wasn't. The last I'd heard of Balls was what Odell had said yesterday, that Balls was off somewhere doing an interview. I wasn't sure at first whether he had spent the night in Manteo or had gone home. But he must have stayed here because he added he was now "finally heading home."

"Got time to swing by here?" I asked, hoping that he would. "Bring me up-to-date."

"Being brought up to date is not part of your job description," he said. Good ol' Balls.

But I sensed he wanted to stop by, maybe chat. I had the uncanny sense there was something he wanted to get off his chest. And I welcomed the opportunity.

Within thirty minutes I heard his Thunderbird rumble up to my carport, swing around, and point nose toward the street.

I stood at the opened kitchen door and watched him lumber up the stairs. His sport shirt was wrinkled, and the top button was undone. He looked weary; so, I pasted a big grin on my face and called out a cheery, "Always great to see you looking so dapper and full of life, Balls."

"Same to you," he mumbled.

I held the storm door open for him. "Want some iced tea?"

"Be great," he said. He settled in the upholstered chair I have near the sliding glass doors. I got his iced tea and then perched for a moment on one of the barstools at the kitchen counter; then I moved on to the sofa and sat there and waited. He sipped his tea and did the thousand-yard stare thing. I waited.

Finally, he spoke. "You can rule out your buddy Schweikert as a possible suspect," he said. "His wife'll alibi him out."

"That's where you've been?"

"Huh?"

"Talking to Schweikert's wife?"

He nodded. "Yeah." His voice trailed off before the one word was fully spoken.

"She say he was there that night with her?" I asked.

Another, "Yeah." But then he took a sip of his tea and said, "She said he was 'here' but not really 'here, here.'"

He glanced at me. A puzzled expression on my face.

"You know what she meant. I did too. She said she watched television alone, as usual, and he stayed in his study all evening, then went to bed while she was watching the eleven o'clock local news." He got that lopsided grin of his. "Said she wanted to see how many shootings there were up in Norfolk. That's why the local news."

"What's she like?"

"Huh?"

"Schweikert's wife. What's she like?"

Balls studied his iced tea as if the answer floated there. Finally, he spoke. "Depressed. Beat down. Wilted, like a flower way past its blooming." He got that big grin of his again—momentarily. "Hey, I'm sounding like one of you writer types. Hanging around you too much."

"You don't peg him as a viable suspect anyway, do you?"

"Naw."

"Me either," I said. "Not if this is a serial killer. And been no link with him and the Ferguson woman, from what I've heard . . . or not heard."

Balls was quiet again. "I didn't even bring up the Trigger Massey business. She did. Said she knew what I was wondering about. Said she knew he was—how'd she put it? —'intimate' with the Massey woman, and others. But a killer, no."

I said, "Not even consensual sex gone bad, which happens sometimes. But without a connection to the other woman, and the similar M.O., kind of rules him out."

Once again, Balls lapsed into silence, that stare off in the great distance returning. I waited. I knew he wanted to talk a bit more. I was going to take advantage of it. Not the usual banter, but something from the depth of his heart, I sensed.

He looked at me, his eyes locked on my face. "I felt sorry for her. I really did. Like life was too much for her." He hesitated again. "Tell you the truth, Weav, in a way she reminded me of Lorraine. I mean depressed and all. Not for the same reason, of course. I ain't doing any afternoon delight stuff, but I'm often not 'here, here,' as Mrs. Schweikert put it." He gave a brief shake of his massive head.

Although it was not the usual Balls I'd grown accustomed to over the years, there were, like this, a few times when he actually revealed himself. This was one of those times. So I remained quiet. Reverent? Well, almost.

"I better get on home," he said.

"Yes."

"And I'm gonna stay there a couple days, at least."

"Good," I said. I didn't know what else to say.

He rose. "Thanks for the iced tea," he said.

I nodded and watched him leave.

The next couple of days blurred by with work on the book, another fairly short assignment from Rose, and emails and phone calls—the sort of thing that tend to make one day meld into another without strong recollection of what happened the day before. By Friday afternoon I realized I hadn't gotten around to picking up that file from Odell.

Did it matter really? I was unlikely to find anything new. It wasn't even my case. And besides, I had other plans. I was really looking forward to Saturday morning.

Elly and I planned to treat Martin and his little friend Lauren from next door to a round of miniature golf. A sort of family outing. These outings were nice. I missed Elly, even though we talked two or three times a day on the phone; but I missed the close proximity we enjoyed in Paris, living together in that apartment.

Ah, yes, No. 8 rue des Grand Degres on the Left Bank. Yes, Harrison, it was like being married. And you know this has got to be fluttering around in your mind more than you admit to yourself. Yes, I know, I know.

Saturday morning was bright and sunny and promised to be another beautiful spring day with light and variable breezes. By nine-thirty I was driving over to Elly's. As I cruised through Manteo, I thought about the courthouse and the rape/murder cases. I had checked daily with Odell or with Balls, making something of a pest of myself. I was used to being a pest, though. Had to chuckle. That's what made me a good reporter—being a pest. Hanging in there, asking questions, one after the other. Even using the "Colombo" tactic of starting to leave and then pretending to remember, "Oh, one more thing . . ."

When I pulled into Elly's gravel driveway, Martin came bounding out the screen door, letting it slam shut behind him. He waited on the front steps, dancing from one foot to the other. Little Lauren came out behind him, opening the screen door and gently closing it. Both, though, had big smiles. Elly, shaking her head in mock frustration was the third person to open the screen door and step out on the porch.

I looked at her with admiration. She and I both wore khaki shorts. My cotton golf shirt was blue and hers was a soft pink. We both wore sockless boat shoes. "Didn't you get the memo about blue shirts?" I said, getting out of the car and approaching the porch.

Her brown hair was pulled back and mostly secured. I wanted to take her and hug her and never let her go, and I think that somehow that message of mine reached her because of the way she looked at me. I think she felt the same way.

Martin and then Lauren ran to my Outback and stood impatiently near the rear doors. Elly approached. I squeezed one of her hands and kissed her discreetly on the side of her lips. She looked up at me, and I loved her very much. It was obvious.

We broke the spell and started to herd the children into the car, but first Elly asked Martin and then Lauren if they wanted to go to the bathroom before we left. They both declined impatiently. Martin had his hands on the door handle. I told him to go ahead and open it and get in and I opened the other side for Lauren. They climbed in as agile as monkeys and began buckling up without having to be told to do so.

Martin and Lauren kept up a steady flow of chatter as we headed toward the beach and one of the miniature golf fixtures on the Bypass.

Elly and I smiled, listening to the lively conversation that came to us from the backseat.

Lauren said, "I'll win again. I know I will."

"You didn't win last time. I did," Martin said.

"No, I did. I had the highest score."

"The highest score loses, dummy."

Elly spoke to Martin. "We don't call people names, Martin."

"All right," he said, but to Lauren he said, "This is golf. You don't know anything about golf."

"I do, too."

"Not like I do," Martin said. With a glance in the rearview mirror, I could see that he squared his shoulders and leaned back in his seat, a commanding expression in his face. "I'm going to be either a famous artist or a famous golfer when I grow up. I know everything about golf."

Certainly not to be outdone, Lauren said, "I'm going to be either a famous dancer or a famous fireman and save babies and puppies and things."

"You're a girl. You can't be a fire*man*. And who ever heard of a fire*woman*?"

Turning my head slightly, I said to Martin, "There are lots of women firefighters today, Martin."

"Just the same . . ." he grumbled.

"See there," Lauren said. While I didn't see it, she probably added an eyeroll.

At the miniature golf facility, there was the usual delay as Martin and Lauren debated with themselves as to what color ball they wanted. Martin finally selected a yellow and Lauren a purple one. Elly and I followed them, and we started. I enjoyed it. Lauren took her time; Martin was a bit more compulsive and whacked the ball entirely too smartly from time to time. When we finished the first round, with the balls disappearing down the final hole, I announced that Martin and Lauren were tied—with good scores—and that they beat both Elly and me.

They wanted to play again. It was not crowded, so I agreed. Elly said she would sit this one out—on a bench placed in the shade of an undernourished little tree off to one side.

When we finished this round, I announced that Martin and Lauren had again tied with what were definitely world-famous scores. They swelled with pride and turned in their clubs.

It was time now for desserts—ice cream and the works.

I walked over to Elly while Martin and Lauren critiqued the playing of three preteens who had started.

Elly looked up with a smile. She held her left hand out on her thigh, fingers spread, tilted her hand from side to side, and went back to looking at her ring. "I've been watching the way the sun catches my ring," she said. "It is really and truly a beautiful ring, Harrison."

The wide gold band, ringed with tiny sapphires and diamonds, sparkled in the sun.

"We've got to figure out what kind of ring it is," I said. I sat beside her on the bench, our shoulders and hips touching. For a moment, she looked puzzled, then gave a knowing smile.

"Yes, we do," she said.

"Whether engagement, special friendship . . . or just a pretty ring."

I think she started saying, "I think we'll know . . ." but Martin and Lauren came rushing up and wanted to know when we were going to get ice cream. I believe Elly was about to say to me, "We'll know soon." But I'm not sure.

We loaded up in the car and went for dessert at one of the frozen yogurt places on the way to Manteo. While Martin and Lauren dug into what they thought was ice cream, Elly only played with hers. She was unusually quiet. I whispered, "Something bothering you?"

She paused a moment, fingering the tall glass of water in front of her. "Well, I've been thinking about those . . . those, you know, two cases. They make me sad, and scared maybe, too." She pursed her lips. "You'd think that something might have, you know, come to light by now . . . some sort of progress."

I didn't know what else to add. So I kept silent.

She looked up at my eyes. There was sorrow in her expression. "I just hope, Harrison, that there doesn't have to be another one before . . . before the person is caught."

"So do I," I said. Then, "Maybe there won't be another one."

She got the sad little smile. "You don't believe that any more than I do."

Chapter Nineteen

Everything was quiet on the case for the next full week, and a day or so starting into the next. Not that efforts weren't made every day. More people interviewed. I kept close contact with Odell—and even bugged Balls a couple of times, though he was trying his best to spend more time at home. Every interrogation and inquiry led nowhere.

Yes, damn it, I'd finally gotten around to going to the courthouse specifically to view those spending records of Trigger and Ferguson's. More frustration.

The most up-to-date records of Trigger's were missing. And, as noted by Odell, the Ferguson woman's files were essentially nonexistent.

I asked Odell about the missing page or pages of Trigger's records.

"Oh, Deputy Phillips got 'em," he said. "She's been going over 'em. Hasn't found anything of interest. But I can get 'em back. No problem."

He referred to Deputy J.R. Phillips, the female deputy whom Odell groomed as an up-and-coming investigator.

We agreed I'd be next.

Okay, but at least my visit gave me an opportunity to chat a moment or two with Elly.

So, progress continued slow, or nonexistent.

But then it happened.

I had gone to eat dinner by myself at Barefoot Bernie's, and I'd taken my time. Even had the latest Lee Child's "Jack Reacher" book with me and managed a few pages of that waiting for my food; more reading off and on during the meal; and then several more pages while I dawdled over coffee at the end of the meal. A habit I picked up a long time ago was to take a book with me virtually every time I went out. Amazing how much reading one could do in doctor's offices, waiting in line for some type of service, alone like tonight in a restaurant, or even during commercials while glued to a television set.

I'd never be able to reach Pat Conroy's goal of reading two hundred pages a day, or the way Thomas Wolfe read with a stopwatch in hand to time how long it took him to read a page. But I never stopped work on reading a lot; and one thing I gave myself credit for was that I often go back over sentences to see how the writer put them together. To savor the flavor of those glowing sentences. To me, that was more important as a writer than simply the number of pages read.

When I finally did leave Barefoot Bernie's and got back home it was close to nine o'clock. The red light on my answering machine blinked. I spoke to Janey in passing and went straight to the phone, after stepping over the neck of the bass fiddle.

I pushed play. I vowed once again to get a more up-to-date answering device.

The call had come in only ten minutes earlier.

A breathless excitement in his voice, it was Dorsey, one of the deputies. "Odell wanted me to alert you. There's been an attempted rape. He and J.R. are on their way to OBX hospital. Where the victim is." He signed off.

I could picture Dorsey's ruddy complexion, made even ruddier with excitement. He worked closely with Odell and was the go-to for photographs. The deputy with Odell was J.R. Phillips, the female investigator. She would be a logical one to accompany him to interview an intended woman rape victim.

Wasting no time, I did a quick brush of my teeth, washed at my face or at least smacked water on it, and started to head out. But the phone rang. Had to be something to do with this latest. I rushed over to grab the phone.

It was Gail Hutchison, Dare County's victim's advocate. "I'm at the emergency room of the hospital," she said. "Here with Lila Quenton, the intended victim . . ."

"Oh, my God," I said, interrupting Gail. An icy wave of apprehension swept over me. "That's terrible. She all right?"

"She was not physically hurt. Emotional trauma, of course. Physically unscathed, thank the Good Lord. Detectives are here. But she wants to talk to you. She told me first thing she wanted to talk to you."

"I'm on my way," I said.

We disconnected and I put Janey's cover partially over her cage. "May be morning before I get back, Janey," I said.

"Shit," she said, before beginning a soft chatter to herself, which she always did when I covered her cage at sleep time. It was her routine of putting herself to sleep, I guess.

I grabbed a light windbreaker, and I was out of there.

I drove faster than I should have, perhaps, but I didn't care. I wanted to get down there and see Lila, make sure she was all right, be there for her. I couldn't but wonder if I'd spent more time bird-dogging this case, I could have prevented this from happening to Lila.

The stoplights favored me—even the one at First Street —and I made excellent time. Swung past Jockey's Ridge pushing more than sixty, well above the posted speed limit of fifty.

I peeled into the driveway of the hospital and went left to park near as I could to the emergency room entrance. Two Nags Head police cruisers were close to the carport, their dome lights still on. A Dare County sheriff's car squeezed in next to the cruisers.

I scurried past a lighted rescue vehicle where two EMTs worked at putting it back in order. An ambulance squatted under the carport at the entrance to the emergency room.

Automatic doors swished open. In the waiting room, two

would-be patients, a hefty woman and a frail looking man, sat side-by-side, watching, with what had to be bewilderment, the frantic coming and going of official personnel.

I went straight to the woman sitting behind the counter. Her face was completely neutral, and so was her voice when she uttered only, "Yes?"

"I'm Harrison Weaver, and Gail Hutchison from Dare County Sheriff's Office said she wanted me to . . ."

Then, off to the right, I saw Gail waving to get my attention. To the woman behind the desk, Gail said, "Would you please let Mr. Weaver enter?"

With what appeared to be reluctance, Ms. Neutral Expression pushed a button, and I heard the door to my left click. "Through there," she said, with the barest tilt of her head.

The triage nurse in the room behind the door gave me a pleasant nod toward a door on the other side of the small room. "You can go right in," she said.

As I neared the door it opened from the other side. Gail stood there, her hand still on the doorknob. My heart beat faster than normal. I inhaled deeply, exhaled, and spoke to Gail.

My words tumbled. "You say Lila is all right? Wasn't hurt?"

"She's not hurt. She's very lucky. Nearly in shock. They're monitoring her closely. Doctor and nurse in there with her right now . . . as are Deputy Wright and the woman deputy."

"Odell Wright is already here? Deputy J.R. Phillips, too?"

"They haven't been here long."

Gail and I stood near the center workstation for the doctors and nurses. Phones rang and two nurses busied with charts and computers. Two Nags Head uniformed officers stood at one end. They watched us.

"Where is she?" I asked Gail.

"There in number four."

The curtain was pulled close. I turned halfway around so I could keep an eye on number four and still talk with Gail.

"How did it happen?" I asked. "And did they catch the guy?"

"She'll tell you, I'm sure," Gail said. "I know the barest of details—that she was able to run out of her house with no clothes on and get the older couple next door to call 911. And, no, the suspect got completely away. There are officers there now scouring the neighborhood . . . but I think the suspect was gone long before they started looking for him . . . and they don't even know who they are looking for."

"No ID, huh?"

"No. He was disguised or something," Gail said.

The ER doctor pulled back the curtain enough to exit, followed by the nurse. Before the nurse pulled the curtain closed again, I caught a glimpse of Odell, who stood near the bed.

Odell and J.R. were in there with the curtain closed for another ten or more minutes. During that time, the nurse, who had been in the room, and a different one also, went in the room for a short period. With the opening and closing of the curtain, I caught sight of a metal stand with an IV attached.

"Probably a saline solution, maybe a sedative," Gail said softly. She had watched too. "They haven't had to give her the 'cocktail' rape victims usually get to prevent STDs, pregnancy, tetanus—since she wasn't actually . . ."

"I guess you got here before Deputy Wright did?" I said.

"Yes. A few minutes before. The sheriff had called me. He's really concerned over these cases. When I got here, two or three uniformed officers were already here, and the rescue squad personnel." She leaned a little closer to keep her voice low. "That's when I was able to talk with her long enough to get the basics and to confirm that she had not been violated —in spirit, yes, but physically no." She tightened her lips.

"She was lucky, very lucky—and plucky, too, and physical enough to get away."

"How did she . . ."

"I'm sure she'll tell you. That's one of the first things she said when I asked her if she wanted me to contact anyone. You know, relatives or someone. She thought for only a moment and then said, 'Harrison Weaver. I want to tell him all of the details. Because he'll remember and he'll help me if I want to write about it later. And I'm going to write about it. Every damn bit of it.'"

That was Lila. A writer to the bone.

Gail gave a short shake of her head. "Lila was very agitated and talking quite fast."

The ER doctor went into number four for a couple of minutes. He came back out and hurried into one of the other cubicles. At ten twenty-two, Odell and J.R. Phillips pulled back the curtain enough to exit number four. Odell nodded toward Gail and me and strode over to where we stood. J.R. was behind him.

After a short greeting, mostly aimed at Gail, Odell said, "J.R. and I are going over to Ms. Quenton's house in Nags Head." Taking me in with a sweep of his eyes, he said, "Deputy Dorsey is there securing the scene." Back to Gail, he said, "J.R. is going to get Ms. Quenton some clothes and bring 'em back here. She doesn't have any clothes . . . with her. We may be a while. The doctor will release her shortly. She's in good shape . . . well, as good a shape as you figure she can be."

Gail spoke up. "I can follow you and bring the clothes back, if you want me to."

"That's okay," J.R. said. "I've told her she can crash at my house tonight. I've got an extra room and she doesn't want to go back to her place tonight, not by herself."

"That's awfully nice of you, deputy." Then to Odell, Gail said, "Ms. Quenton said she wanted to talk with Mr. Weaver."

Odell managed a quick wry half-smile. "Yeah, that's what she said. One writer to another sort of thing." He shook his head, but his eyes crinkled with a touch of humor.

Odell and J.R. left, and Gail said, "I'll go in there with you, and stay the full time. She'll be wanting to talk mostly with you. I know the doctor is ready to release her, but she's not going anywhere right away—not until she gets some clothes and Deputy Phillips returns."

"Let's go in," I said, and we went toward cubicle number four.

Chapter Twenty

Gail and I pulled back the curtain to number four and went inside. Lila lay with her eyes closed. She opened them when we came in. She managed a smile. A weak smile, it's true, but a smile nonetheless. She nodded something of a greeting.

The IV stand stood close to the head of her bed. Whatever had been in the IV bag appeared to have been depleted. She was covered with a sheet and a light tan blanket. I could see her shoulders, and I could tell she had on two of the faded blue hospital gowns. A nurse, or someone, had kindly considered her modesty. One of the gowns, I knew, opened in the back, and the other opened in the front. This way she didn't get out in the hall or somewhere and have her rear shining for all to see.

I lightly took one of her hands momentarily. "Hello, Lila."

Again, she tried a smile. "Right now, I really do feel like one of those 'ink-stained wretches' you always mention when describing those of us who strive to . . . to write."

Lila's lips were pale and parched. Her hair was pushed forward by the pillow. Above her left cheek, there was a small red mark, maybe the start of a bruise. It wasn't too bad. She still looked good.

I smiled and nodded. "You've earned it," I said.

Gail stepped closer. "I brought with me one of the Sexual Assault Evidence Collection Kits—or rape kits, as they're called—but as you indicated initially, I don't think we need to . . . you know, I don't think it's needed since . . ."

"No," Lila said, "the son-of-a-bitch didn't . . . and the

way I kicked him, it may be quite a while before he tries something again. The bastard."

Gail said, "I've told the SANE nurse that we won't be needing her." The acronym stood for the specially trained Sexual Assault Nurse Examiner.

With the tips of my fingers, I rubbed the top of Lila's wrist. "And no ID? You couldn't see him, his face?"

"Like I told Gail and the deputy—the nice African-American and the woman detective—he had on a disguise—a false face. One of those things that covers the entire head, like Halloween or something . . ."

"She's a deputy," I said.

"What?"

"The woman with Chief Deputy Odell Wright is another deputy. Not a detective, but she's very good."

"Nice, too," Lila said. "She's bringing me clothes . . . and I'm going to her house tonight."

Gail said, "Yes, that is very thoughtful of her," To me, she said, "I told Lila that Hot Line has a rolling cart here with extra sweatpants and tops in all sizes, and she'd be welcome . . . but she wanted her own clothes from home, and I understand."

Lila smiled at her. "That's right, but I thank you. You've been very supportive and kind. Understanding."

Gail said, "And I'll be with you tomorrow when Deputy Wright and maybe others want to do a more in-depth interview."

Then turning her face to me, Lila said, "I said I wanted to talk to you because I want to write about this later, and you can help me remember what I say tonight and help me edit it." She shook her head and managed the saddest of smiles very briefly. "Not exactly in a position to write down my thoughts now—and probably not capable of it, either."

I said, "Why don't you tell me, right from the start, as if you're writing it down. I'll remember. I'm good at it. Maybe not as good as Truman Capote claimed he was in gathering interviews for *In Cold Blood*. But after all, Capote was a fiction writer—and a damn good one—and like all fiction writers, he sometimes had trouble distinguishing between what really transpired with what had happened only in his imagination."

"Okay," Lila said. "Let me tell you, right from the beginning."

Gail said, "I'll sit over here in the corner and listen."

"Sure," Lila said.

Two utilitarian chairs were pushed against a far wall. Gail took one and pulled it farther to the side. I moved the other one closer to the bed and sat beside Lila.

Lila turned her head toward me. "Okay, put that memory notepad of yours to work." Again that weak smile. She was a pretty lady, even under these conditions.

"Memory notepad engaged," I said.

"I was home, alone, as always, and I'd just finished watching *Jeopardy*—and I got the final answer. Lady Brett was a character in Hemingway's *The Sun Also Rises*—when there was a knock on the front door. A polite knock. The doorbell doesn't work part of the time. I didn't think much of it. Probably still half watching the TV, I went to the door. Flipped on the porch light, I think. Yes, I remember I did. Because it was dark. *Jeopardy* was recorded so I could play it later than seven-thirty.

"There was this tall guy standing there—still halfway in the dark. The porch light isn't that much. He had his back to me and had a windbreaker on and was wearing a slouch hat. Not exactly an Indiana Jones hat, but one like it.

"To tell the truth, Weav, I first thought it was one of the guys from the open mic/critique group. I wouldn't have started to open the door otherwise. The real tall one—and I can't remember his name—but he has sort of been, I don't know, overly attentive, friendly. Nothing out of the way, but, you know, I could tell that any relaxation or encouragement on my part and—and well, you know."

She took a shallow breath. "Then he turned around when I opened the door fully—and I did a real double-take because he had on one of those full-head rubber faces. It wasn't a Richard Nixon face, but it was something like that."

I raised the palm of one hand a few inches, and she stopped, waiting for me. "How frightened were you right in the beginning?"

"You know, it's a funny thing, I was startled. That's true, but I wasn't all that scared. Not in the beginning." She gave a tiny shake of her head.

"It wasn't someone from the writers' group, though?" I said.

"Oh, no, no indeed. I remember I said something like, 'Hey, it isn't even Trick or Treat night. Something like that. Blowing it off." A slight shudder coursed through her body. I sensed that Gail leaned forward because she saw it too. Lila's voice took on a more somber tone. Her facial expression shifted, too.

Lila continued, her eyes trained steadily on mine. "Suddenly, I knew something was wrong. This wasn't the guy from the writers' group. I really don't know whether it was something he said or did or what. But suddenly I knew. This wasn't right, and I felt terror . . . real terror . . . and coldness. I remember there was coldness, and I believe I started trembling. I'm sure I did. But I just stood there and he stepped closer, and I backed up and he put his hand on the doorknob so I couldn't shut the door and I looked at his hand—it was his right hand—and he had on a blue latex glove."

Her words came faster. Lila still stared at me, but it was as if she was watching a video of what she said and what she recalled. It was not me she looked at; it was a moving image spinning out for her to see as she talked.

She said, "He may have pushed me with his hand. No, I don't think so because that one hand held open the door and his other hand was still in his windbreaker jacket . . ."

I held a palm up again. "You mentioned the windbreaker

and the hat. What else was he wearing?"

"He had on regular khaki slacks, a pullover shirt, and that bulky windbreaker . . . and his false face and hat." She took a shallow breath before continuing. "Then he said, 'Get back in,' or something like that—and his voice, his voice, it was scary sounding . . ."

"Would you recognize his voice again?" I asked.

"No, no. It was not a normal voice. It was like it was mechanical or something. It wasn't like, you know, Darth Vader, but it was that kind of sound. Like maybe he had something in his mouth or throat that distorted his voice." She shook her head and shuddered again. I patted her wrist.

"It was then that he . . . that he told me to get inside and at the same time he pulled out his left hand and he had a gun, holding a gun in his hand that had a blue latex glove like his other hand."

"What kind of gun?" I asked. "I don't mean the make. But was it a handgun? Pistol or revolver? Big or little?"

"It seemed big to me, but maybe it wasn't. It was not long, I mean not like in a cowboy movie. That's a revolver, isn't it? The cowboy guns?"

"Yes," I said. "It was probably a pistol." Then I added, "This is information you told Deputy Wright and J.R., isn't it?"

She nodded. "Not in as much detail. But these basic facts."

"Go on," I said.

"With that gun pointed at me, he told me again to get inside. He said, 'Now. Right now.' And I started backing up, still looking at him, or looking at that gun, I don't remember which."

Lila stopped talking as a nurse came in. It was one of the nurses who had been in earlier. "I'll unhook your IV," the nurse said. I scooted my chair back so the nurse could move around the bed if she needed to. "You're not in the way," the nurse said.

The nurse eased the needle out of the top of Lila's left hand, secured the IV, and wheeled the stand out of the room.

Lila said, "Inside the foyer, he shoved that gun against my chest, and said for me to go back to the bedroom. That voice. It was an awful voice, and it scared me as much as the gun. At least that's the way I remember it. Scary sounding." She shook her head again, reliving the memory.

"Next thing—I don't even remember going back there—we were in the bedroom and I was standing near the foot of the bed."

"Where was he?" I said. "What was he doing?"

"He was just . . . just standing there, I think. And then that voice said, 'Take your clothes off.' I didn't move. I may have said no or something like that because that's when he hit me."

I could see from the corner of my eyes that Gail sat on the edge of her chair, leaning forward, her hands folded tightly together.

"He hit you?" I said. "With his hand?"

"No," she said, "with the gun." With the fingers of her now-free left hand, she lightly touched the red spot on her cheekbone.

"Then he pointed that gun at me. Held it real close. He said, 'Do what I tell you or I'll kill you right now.'" She fought to control her emotions as she talked. Her breathing was very deliberate.

I waited. I sensed that Gail was about to say something, so I spoke up. "If this is too much for you right now, Lila, we can do it later."

With her chin raised slightly, she shook her head. "No, no. I want to get it out now."

Gail eased back in her chair.

"Okay," I said. "Memory notepad engaged."

"So I started to . . . to take my clothes off."

"What were you wearing?"

"I was not dressed up much, you know. I'd gotten comfortable when I got home. A long-sleeve cotton pullover. Tailored elastic-topped sweatpants, the kind you can wear to the grocery store, floppy socks, and old sneakers. And underwear, of course."

I held my palm up, and she waited for me to speak. "Now this can be important in this overall investigation, and the other cases as well. Please try to remember exactly what he was doing while you . . . while you started to get undressed. And how did you do that? What did you take off first, and what did he do?"

Lila said, "Well, first I pulled my top up over my head, and then . . . but before I put the top on the bed, he told me to fold it neatly, and lay it in the chair, carefully. And I did that. He was still holding that gun in his hand, but with his other hand—and I could tell he was really looking at me, despite that rubber face—he began to sort of rub or massage his . . . lower stomach. Well, you know, actually his groin area."

"But he had you fold your top and put it on the chair?"

When she told about neatly folding the piece of clothing, I cast a quick glance at Gail. She gave the slightest nod of her head. She knew about the neatly folded clothes that had been found at the two other crime scenes.

Chapter Twenty-One

Lila said, "Yes, he made me fold the top and put it neatly on the chair near the foot of the bed. Then I guess I kicked off my sneakers. Probably. He motioned with the gun for me to keep on going, undressing. And I hooked my thumbs in the top of my sweatpants . . . but he stopped me and said for me to put the shoes under the chair, lined up. Then he told me to take off my socks and fold them, put them on the chair."

I held my hand up again. "Lila, tell me, best you can, what you were feeling at the time . . . while he's making you undress, and what he was doing." She acquiesced with the barest movement of her head. "I'm asking you to go into such detail, Lila, because it will help you remember when you start to write, but it's something I need to hear, and Gail needs to hear while it is all so fresh in your mind. There may be things that you don't think are all that relevant but aid in the overall investigation." I tried for a self-effacing smile, "And believe it or not, I'm not asking for details out of some sort of prurient fascination."

"I know," she said. She stared off in the distance for a moment or two. "To tell you the truth, I was not thinking as much about what he might do to me—I figured it was sex—but I was thinking about how I might get away. I mean he was tall and probably strong maybe, but I knew too that I was fast, and I was thinking about that." She shook her head. "At the same time, I was scared. I tried to tell myself not to be so scared that I couldn't do anything. Kept telling myself to look for a way to escape." Again, a shake of the head. "Leastwise, that's what I think now that I was thinking about then."

I said, "Okay, you took off your socks and folded them and placed them on the chair."

"Yes," she said, "and then with that creepy voice he said for me to keep on going. I could tell, despite that voice, that he was enjoying this. Bastard."

"You still had on your sweatpants," I said. It was not a question. It was a prompt.

She nodded. "Yes, sweatpants. And my bra. I still had on my bra. He made a motion with the gun to keep going. Undressing. I remember I took a really deep breath and hooked my thumbs in the elastic waistband of the sweatpants . . . and began to move them down, step out of them without sitting on the end of the bed or falling over."

Then I said, "Could you see his eyes? I know you couldn't see his face. But his eyes? He was looking at you. Could you see his eyes? The color?"

"No, except that they were dark. Probably brown. Yes, probably brown. Because they weren't bright, you know like blue or something." She stopped again, thinking, remembering. "I tried not to look at that face . . . or to hear that voice. But I did see his eyes, or see them a little bit. But I didn't look at them long."

After letting her pause, I prompted, "You managed to get out of your sweatpants without falling over or sitting on the bed?"

"Yes, and he motioned for me to fold them and lay them with the top . . . so I'm just standing there, trying to figure out how I can make a break or something. I knew if I tried to run, he'd reach out and grab me before I could get past him to the door . . . or he'd shoot me."

I said, "You're standing there? You still have on your . . . your underwear?"

"Yes. I have on my bra and panties. He points the end of the gun at the bra and moves his head up and down, telling me to take off the bra, but without saying anything." She tilt-

ed her head. "I don't know, of course, but he may have had
trouble keeping that mechanical voice going. Maybe it was
not all that comfortable or something." A shake of her head.
"I didn't want to hear that voice anyway."

Lila flicked her tongue across her lips. "Water? Could I
have some water?"

Gail started to get up, but I reached the glass that was
mostly full. It had a bent straw in it. "It's not cold," I said,
moving the glass toward her. I helped her support the glass,
and with the other hand I steadied her neck and head.

"Thanks," she said. Another hesitation. "So I took off
my bra, and he motioned with the gun to put it with the other
things. I folded it and laid it on top of the sweatpants and
socks."

For the first time, she got what had to be an expression of
embarrassment. I could tell she was trying to form her next
statement. "Then he . . . he pushed his pants down. I don't
know whether he had underwear on or not but if he did, he
pushed his underwear down at the same time he pushed his
pants down. Down to his ankles. Bunched up there. And he's
standing there with that Halloween face and slouch hat and
some sort of sweatshirt that barely reaches his waist and
those pants bunched up at his ankles, and he looks . . ."

She stared up at me as if to gauge how I would react to
her next statement. "He looked really funny, you know, com-
ical. Ridiculous. Like something out of a comic movie or
something."

"I got the picture," I said, and tried to conceal a growing
smile. But that momentary image of a comic situation faded
quickly. No smile from me. This was a potentially lethal situation. Nothing funny about that.

"And there I am standing there in nothing but my panties. He motions for me to take my panties off." Again she
stopped. I waited. "Weav, he's there in all of his . . . his inglorious condition."

"Inglorious condition?" I said.

"Yes. You know, he was not at all excited. He was not . . . you know . . ."

"Yes, I know," I said.

"And I took my panties off. I started folding them to put with the other things, and he said, 'No, give them to me.' I hesitated maybe a second or two and he said it again with that voice. I handed him my panties and he held them there in his free hand, and he squeezed them or worked them in his hand." She stared at me a moment, then averted her eyes. "Now, suddenly, he was all excited . . . erect." She turned her head toward the water glass. I held it for her. She took a thirsty pull on the straw.

"He bent his knees," she said, "like he was almost squatting to reach his pants. I sat down on the edge of the bed, partly to sort of hide myself. He fumbled with his pants, trying to put my panties in his pocket."

She took a deep breath. "He finally managed to get my panties in his pocket, and he started to stand back up."

Her chin thrust out, Lila said, "He was still partly bent over, his knees apart—and that's when I knew I had to make my move."

I leaned forward, and I sensed Gail did the same. Listening intently.

Lila said, "I kicked out with my right foot. I kicked really, really hard . . . and I've got strong legs from all the running and everything. My foot hit him right between the legs. Right where I wanted to hit the bastard.

"He made a loud sound, like a moan or groan or something. Making that sound, his voice was more like a regular voice. Not mechanical. But not human sounding either." She searched for a word. "Maybe like an animal?"

Lila saw that Gail and I both waited. "Anyway, he doubled up. Almost sitting on his heels. With the same foot, I pushed it right into his Halloween face as hard as I could. Really hard, and he went tumbling over backwards and I jumped up and ran. I've never run faster. I may have even leaped over him. I'm not sure. But I was out of there and racing toward the front door."

I gave Lila another sip of water.

"As I reached the front door, I heard the gun go off. Real loud. It may have gone off twice, real quick, together, or maybe an echo or something. But I knew it hadn't hit me. I wasn't shot."

Softly, Gail said, "The ceiling and bed. One round in the ceiling and one in the end of the bed. That's what Nags Head officers came back and told Deputy Wright."

Lila listened to Gail, and then nodded. "I kept running. Out the front door. I may have slammed it shut. I don't remember." She motioned for the water again. After another sip, she said, "I do remember that outside I paused a millisecond, looking right and left, which way to run. There are vacant lots on each side of my house. Nothing much on the right. Mostly stubby little bushes and weeds. To the left there's the Pressley house beyond the vacant lot. I ran that way. Toward the Pressley house."

Lila took a deep breath. I put my hand on the water glass, but she gave a jerky shake of her head. "Barefooted . . . and naked. Mainly I remember how my feet hurt. But I really ran fast. I didn't care."

She stopped again, as if gathering her thoughts, trying to remember details, how she felt. "I think I may have been crying as I ran. I may have been. It seems like I was, but I could see the Pressley house real clearly, so my eyes weren't, you know, clouded up with tears."

During the pause, Gail said, "Did they look at your feet? The doctor? Nurse?"

Lila moved her feet under the sheet. "Yes. There were a couple of small cuts or more like scratches, but nothing serious. They put some medicine on them . . . my feet, and socks."

"You made it to the Pressley's house," I prompted.

"Yes." That half-smile. "Probably broke a speed record.

I pounded on their door. They're a retired couple, older. I may have rung the doorbell too, but I remember smacking this hand hard on the door. Pounding." She held up her right hand; then put it back on the bed and I touched it lightly.

"All that pounding probably scared them out of their wits. It wasn't all that late . . . just the same." Lila gave a shake of her head. "Mrs. Pressley came to the door, opened it—and her mouth—at the same time. She looked me up and down, put a hand to her mouth, and said something like, 'My God, child. What happened to you?' And then right behind her came old Mr. Pressley. He may have said something also, but the first thing he did was grab a raincoat off the peg there in the hallway. At first it looked like he was going to give it to me. Instead, he gave it to Mrs. Pressley, and she gave it to me. I held it in front of myself. Didn't put it on right away, just held it there."

"You were still standing outside by the front door?" I said.

"Yes, but this is only seconds. At the same time, I was screaming out to call 911, call the police . . . there's a man in my house." Mrs. Pressley motioned for me to come in. Of course, by then the bastard was gone, I'm sure. He probably left as soon as he could straighten up, stand up."

Lila said, "I turned my back to Mr. and Mrs. Pressley and put the raincoat on. It was way too big, but it sure covered me." Lila stopped talking and looked around the room. "The raincoat?" she said.

"The deputy took it. Said she'd give it back to the people next door," Gail said.

"It couldn't have been long. A few minutes maybe, and I heard police sirens and the rescue squad. Seems like there were a dozen police officers. I'm sure there weren't that many. They went all over my house and the yard and the rescue man and woman put me in the ambulance . . . and here I am."

"You did a great job of describing what happened, Lila.

And I'll remember it, and so will you, I'm certain . . . and you'll be able to write it all, and then some."

It wasn't long before the curtain was pulled back and Deputy J.R. Phillips entered. She carried a tote bag. "I brought you clothes," J.R. said. "Not sure it's what you wanted, but it's clothes, shoes, socks and . . . and under-wear." Then with a glance toward me, J.R. said, "We had to leave the clothes you were wearing, folded up on the chair."

"Anything is good," Lila said. "Thank you so very much."

Gail and I both stood, perhaps somewhat awkwardly be-cause we didn't know what was next. It seemed like time to go.

J.R. said, "I'm off for tonight. Deputy Wright and some others are still at your house, but they'll be leaving soon, and securing it good. They'll post someone there all night."

"No sign of that bastard?" Lila's voice was strong.

J.R. shook her head. "Nags Head uniforms are still searching. But no."

"He surely had his car near there someplace," I said. "And he took off . . . soon as he was able."

Lila gave me that wry half-smile, probably thinking of the powerful kick she had administered to his groin.

Under her breath, Lila muttered, "Bastard."

A nurse came in with discharge papers for Lila. "You're free to go, soon as this paperwork is finished."

"And I can take you on to my place," J.R. said. Then she added, "Deputy Wright and maybe the SBI want to talk with you tomorrow. We can do that at the courthouse at nine."

"Okay," Lila said. Her tone was flat, weariness begin-ning to creep in.

"Afterwards, I can take you to your house, or wherever you want to go."

"Fine," Lila said. She swung her legs around to the edge of the bed and tugged upward on the shoulder of one of the gowns.

I said goodnight and that I might see her at the court-house tomorrow, and I left the two women in there with Lila so she could get dressed.

I knew I would definitely see her tomorrow at the court-house. No way was I going to miss that.

Chapter Twenty-Two

By the time I got home and settled in, it was pushing midnight.

On my answering machine, I heard a gruff voice mail message from Balls. He said he would meet me at Henry's for a quick breakfast at seven-thirty before going to the courthouse. He didn't even take time to tell me I'd pay.

When I folded up in the bed, it took a while to get to sleep because I kept replaying Lila's account of her traumatic encounter over in my mind. There would be so much to talk about with Balls and Odell tomorrow.

The next morning a little before seven-thirty I had driven up to Henry's and stood on the front porch waiting for Balls. Within a minute or two he pulled in, parked in the back and shortly he came scowling up. As a way of greeting, he said, "Why haven't you got us a place yet and already ordered?"

"I figured maybe you were on a diet and didn't want anything but a watercress salad."

He frowned at me. "I don't even know what the hell watercress is. Do you?"

We went inside and when the waitress approached, he ordered his loaded three-egg omelet, large tomato juice with crushed ice, double order of white toast, bacon on the side. I ordered a scaled-back version of the same thing.

Balls was quiet while we waited for our food. It came promptly. He was still silent. Uncharacteristic. Finally, with his mouth full, he said, "Okay, give me the bare essentials." He swallowed. "We'll go over details with Odell. No sense in doing it twice . . . three times, or whatever."

I gave him a synopsis of what Lila Quenton had related. I thought he might ask questions during my narrative, but he didn't. He did slow down on his eating, somewhat. When I was finished, he took the last sip of his tall glass of tomato juice, crunched loudly on the ice, and stared at me. He nodded once. "Good," he said. "We'll fill in some details with Odell before the deputy gets there with the woman, the victim."

The waitress got my signal and brought the check. I picked it up. Balls said, "Let's go." Before he got up, though, he looked at my plate. "You gonna eat that last piece of bacon?"

I shook my head.

He picked up the bacon, crammed it in his mouth, made a passing attempt to wipe his fingers on the crumpled napkin, and stood.

Outside, he didn't pause. Over his shoulder he said, "Take both cars. See you there."

This was the all-business Balls. No nonsense. Bearing down. On the scent. As I got in my car, I thought how I'd hate to be a crook and have Balls zeroing in on me. Relentless. You wouldn't have a chance.

At the courthouse I met Elly as she was coming to work. She glanced both ways up and down the hall and gave me quick kiss on the lips. "See you later," she said.

I went upstairs. Balls and Odell were in Odell's office. I took the extra chair. Odell smiled a brief greeting, but they didn't stop their conversation, and I was silent.

Balls rubbed a big paw of a hand across his face. "Different M.O.? Same guy?" He shook his head in what had to be frustration. "Different wrinkles from what we've been thinking."

Odell said, "The disguise . . . the gun . . . We've been figuring it was someone they knew or at least trusted . . ."

I squirmed in my chair. Couldn't keep quiet any longer.

They looked at me, obviously sensing that I was going to say something. "All this doesn't mean it's not the same guy. Maybe he hasn't changed his M.O.—his modus operandi—at all. May be just the same. Or could be a slightly different . . . different style from what we've supposed."

"True," Odell said.

Balls looked at me, face neutral. Cop eyes.

I continued. "Basic neatness freak quirks the same. The folded clothes. Panties as souvenirs." I leaned forward. "Maybe the killing was not part of the plan. The disguise indicates that he didn't want to be recognized. The changed voice. Maybe the killing came because they did do something, or he did something, that made them recognize him . . . or maybe it was part of the enhanced orgasm thing . . . strangling them at the point of his orgasm . . . or maybe trying to get them to orgasm." I settled back. "I don't know. But I think it's the same guy."

They were both silent for at least a full minute. Then Balls said, "Yeah, I think it's the same guy."

Odell nodded, watching Balls, then me, and back to Balls.

Again there was silence. Odell was the first to speak. "Latex gloves. Condom in the first two cases. He sure didn't want to leave any physical evidence."

"And he sure didn't," Balls said.

We heard conversation out in the hall. "They're here," Odell said. "We're set up in the interrogation room." He tilted his head toward the far wall. The interrogation room was next door.

The three of us stood.

Balls looked at me. "Don't you have something else to do?"

Odell raised a palm. "Well, Agent Twiddy, Ms. Quenton likes to talk to Weaver . . ."

"He can come in later," Balls said. "Let's get started with her first."

"That's fine," I said, a bit testily.

Odell pointed to two files on his desk. "I've got those household expenses back from J.R., the ones you wanted to look through. If you want to . . ."

Odell's door opened. In the hall I could see Deputy J.R. Phillips, Gail Hutchison, and Lila.

"Next door," Odell said to J.R.

She nodded, "Yes, sir. Chairs?"

"I dragged in two more earlier," Odell said. He had come from around his desk.

Lila, standing there dressed in sweatpants and a loose-fitting top, appeared smaller than she had looked lying in the hospital bed. She stood a little to one side. She tried to paste a smile on her face from time to time, but the smiles kept fading. I moved a bit closer to the door jamb and to Lila. She said, "Are you coming in? Will you be there?"

"I'll be in after a few minutes," I said.

"Please," she said.

I know Balls and Odell heard her. Surely paved the way for me to enter the interrogation room after they'd had a chance to talk a bit first, to hear her story. Gail's being there would help too.

They moved into the interrogation room. I heard chairs scraped into place as they settled in. Deputy J.R. Phillips remained outside. I went around behind Odell's desk and prepared to go through the household expense files. J.R. came to the door and stepped one foot inside.

I looked up at her. "Go okay last night?"

"Yes, fine," she said. "Nice lady." For one of the first times, J.R. actually grinned at me. "She surely thinks you're great. Best ever."

"I think she's great also."

Before leaving, and getting her neutral, no-nonsense cop look again, there was one more quick grin. "As you say in the South, she thinks you're the greatest thing since sliced bread." And she was gone.

I sat at Odell's desk chair, took a deep breath or sigh, and began flipping open the folders with household expenses, receipts, and appointments for Francine Ferguson and Trigger Massey. Francine's folder was by far the skimpiest. Looking through it, I found very little that was revealing—other than two or three bills marked "overdue."

Next, I opened Trigger's folder. Of course, after she was killed, Odell had instructed deputies to gather up the business receipts and appointments. She had certainly kept meticulous records of expenditures, and other items. She paid all her bills by the due date or before.

In chronological order, starting with the oldest and working my way through to closer to the date when she was murdered, I was nearing the end when I saw something that sent a chill down my spine.

A week before her death, Trigger had received service from, and paid that day, the pest control company: Bugs Away.

The same company whose van had been parked in front of Francine Ferguson's house a short time before she was murdered.

This was enough. Plenty. I closed Trigger's file and sat there a minute. I wanted to compose my questions to Lila. Always best to know exactly what you want to ask and how you want to ask it. The other thing you are supposed to know before you ask a question is the answer. A good interrogator or good attorney wants to know the answer before he or she asks the question. In this instance, I could fashion the question, but there was no way I could know the answer. Only keep my fingers crossed.

I opened the door to the interrogation room as quietly as possible. I caught glances up at me, but Lila—after only the slightest pause—continued with her narrative. She was at the part where she'd kicked the guy in the groin.

I slipped onto the empty seat beside Odell. Balls sat on the other side of Odell, directly across from Lila. Gail had pulled one of the chairs over next to Lila. So the two women on one side of the table, and now, with me, three men on the other side.

To Lila, Balls said, "You say his voice sounded different when he moaned out . . . after you'd kicked him?"

"Yes, sir. It was not mechanical sounding. But it wasn't really human-sounding either. It was more like . . . like an animal or something."

"High pitched or low?"

"High, I think." She paused a moment, her brow wrinkled. "I didn't pay that much attention, except to hear it. That's when I ran, made my escape."

Balls nodded. Then he leaned forward and looked over at me. I had shifted somewhat, and had my hands clasped together in front of me on the table. He knew I wanted to speak.

I said, "I think I know where you live, Lila. Nags Head?"

"Yes."

"Close to the water?"

"Yes. Fairly close. I can see the water."

Balls gave me a puzzled look. So did Odell.

"So do I," I said. "Fairly close." I shifted in my seat and turned my palms upward. "Like everyone else here on this sand bar, I have trouble with so-called water bugs."

Lila gave a tiny wry smile. "They can call them water bugs all they want to. I think they are roaches."

With a half-smile, Gail agreed, "They are. That's exactly what they are."

Balls settled back a bit. So did Odell. They knew I wasn't asking just to make conversation. So they waited.

"We keep the pest control companies in business," I said. I tried to make it sound matter-of-fact. Conversational. Balls knew it wasn't.

"I guess we do," Lila said. "I had a bug company last week."

Trying to keep excitement out of my voice, I said, "Who was that? Who did you use?"

"Oh, the owner had come by several days before. Said he was soliciting business. Gave me one of his cards. Seemed like a nice guy. Very polite and everything. So I made an appointment."

She appeared curious about my questioning, but she continued. "His worker came by last week, as I said." Then she seemed to grasp perhaps why I was asking. A look of concern clouded her face. "He was a big guy. The worker. He didn't say much . . . but he was a big guy. Long arms, big hands." The expression of concern began to grow. "He was a big guy . . ." Her voice trailed off.

Then Lila said, "Why are you asking? I mean, this business about bug companies?"

"Oh, just making conversation," I said.

"I don't believe that," she said, with a fleeting smile. "You don't 'just make conversation.'"

I shrugged and prompted, "The name of the company?"

Her eyes never left mine. I could sense attentive tension from the others. "It was a funny name," she said. "Something like Bugs Be Gone or . . . no, it was Bugs Away. That was it. Bugs Away."

I forced myself to break eye contact, and stare down at my hands.

Chapter Twenty-Three

"Just what the hell was that all about, you wrinkled up ol' bastard?" Balls and I stood in Odell's office, almost nose-to-nose. His tone was gruff and menacing, but I knew Balls well enough to know there was no real animosity involved.

There were the three of us there: Balls, me, and Odell. We had just left the interrogation room. I shrugged and started saying, "I was just making . . ."

"Don't hand me any of that crap," he said. "A dirty-neck newspaper guy like you don't say things 'just making conversation.' Like the lady said, I know there was something you were getting at." He tried his best to scowl, but a touch of—what was it, admiration?—crept to the corner of his eyes. "Weav, never try to bullshit an old bullshitter. You know better 'n that."

Odell stood behind his desk, a soft grin at the exchange. "I think I know," he said. He touched a finger to Trigger's file I'd left open on his desk. "The pest control company. Bugs Away. I know two of the women used the same outfit."

"All three did," I said.

Balls didn't register surprise. He had to know it was something like that. Taking one of Odell's chairs, he slouched there chewing on his lower lip, thinking. I took the other chair and waited.

From the hall, I heard Gail talking with Lila. Gail had offered Lila more assistance, and Lila thanked her and said something about another night at Deputy J.R. Phillips' place. I knew forensic technicians were going over Lila's house—and almost assuredly coming up with nothing. Gail and Lila were walking away but I did hear Lila say a girlfriend of hers would stay with her later at her house.

Balls trained his eyes on me. "I know you," he said, "and I know what you're thinking—but you stay the hell away from that company, that Bugs Aplenty, or whatever it's called."

"Bugs Away," I said.

"Whatever. Stay away." He pursed his lips, smoothed his moustache with the fingers of one big hand. "Let me do some checking."

I tried to relax and look casual. "Well, I do have to get rid of some water bugs . . ."

"You wait a while," he said.

I didn't commit.

Odell took his seat. "Weav *is* a homeowner, and near the water, and . . ."

"I'll do some checking," Balls repeated.

Maybe Balls did think I would stay away. Down deep, though, I don't believe he did. He knew I couldn't resist. After all, it did make sense that I would call on a pest control company since I was a homeowner, with a house not too far from the water.

Balls and Odell said they were going to Lila's house to be with the forensic techs as they finished their work. See if they had found anything, and go over the scene by themselves. I knew they were never satisfied with the work others did; this was especially true of Balls, and he made it known. I suspected Odell felt the same, but he was much more circumspect in expressing his opinions.

They made it clear they didn't want me tagging along.

I went downstairs to see Elly.

Elly and coworker Becky stood at the counter chatting with each other. No one else was there. They saw me coming down the stairs and Becky said, "Here comes Someone Special, Elly."

"Hello, Becky," I said. I reached atop the counter and

held Elly's fingers.

She smiled warmly at me, and then looked down at our hands. With the thumb of her left hand, she touched her ring, there on the third finger. It was almost a caressing touch with her thumb, and something of a twirling motion applied to the ring.

I looked at the ring, too. I said, "We need to make a decision . . . about that ring."

Again, that warm smile. Her eyes felt like they touched mine. A softness, but intense. There was love there. I wanted to hold her, tightly, never let her go.

"Yes," she whispered. "And we will."

We both knew what we were thinking about: was the ring more than an expression of love? We'd both more or less skirted around these questions, as if we weren't sure of ourselves, or weren't sure of the other person. We were both uneasy about it, and maybe our feelings varied from day to day. I'm sure they did. But I knew, too, there was a growing love between us. The fact that both of us had lost through death our previous spouses, was probably another factor that gave us pause, even if a rational person would say it shouldn't.

Elly lost her young husband, a classical-trained and talented cellist, to an especially virulent type of flu. He had never been a very healthy person, Elly said. His death had occurred shortly after she graduated from Meredith College in Raleigh, where he too had been a student. She was pregnant with Martin when her husband died.

For my wife, Keely, it had been a more prolonged thing. She was a musician, also, a pianist who played jazz totally by ear, but mostly she was a hell of a good vocalist. She and I played together in some of the jazz groups around Raleigh and later in Northern Virginia. But always she had had periods of depression. They began to get worse and more prolonged. Eventually she went into deep depression where no one could reach her. Nothing helped, or seemed to. Then one afternoon I came home to find her curled up in bed—where she had been spending days on end. But this time I couldn't wake her. She was dead. Pills. A lot of them. As soon as I'd touched her, I had known she was dead.

I remembered again the total inanimate feel of her body. Like touching a semi-soft statue, but a statue nonetheless. Her suicide left me devastated for weeks, and then months. Much of that time was an alcohol-induced blur for me. It reached the point that now I'm afraid to drink even a beer. I feared that I had crossed some invisible line. And there was never any going back; as the song says, "Through a door marked nevermore."

Becky, to her credit, sensed something private was going on between Elly and me. So she pretended to suddenly become busy straightening three of the large record books.

Elly and I broke our—what was it, really?—emotional embrace, and she said, her tone level, "How did it go upstairs?"

"Oh, fine," I said. Maybe a shrug would end any further inquiry. Fat chance.

Elly said, "Come on, Harrison. I know you better than that. I can tell by looking at you that something's up."

"It's my boyish countenance," I said. Then, with a sidewise grin, "Despite the fact that Balls calls me a wrinkled up ol' bastard." The grin got bigger. "And a dirty-neck newspaper guy."

"I've heard you call yourself that," she said, returning my grin.

"I've also described myself as an ink-stained wretch. Doesn't mean other people ought to call me that."

She cocked one eyebrow. "Okay, you going to tell me what's up?"

I got more serious. "Not yet. You know I will. But not yet." I studied an imaginary spot on the counter. "And it may be nothing. Nothing at all."

Now Elly touched my hands, a light squeeze from her

fingers. "Be careful. Please, please be careful."

"Oh, it's nothing like that . . . I mean that might lead to . . . oh, nothing like that."

"Uh-huh. Right. I've heard that before."

A paralegal came in, a post-college age young woman I'd seen before. Becky said, "Can I help you?"

As the paralegal spoke to Becky, I told Elly I would check with her later.

"Coming to the house tonight?" she said.

"That would be lovely," I said.

"Supper," she said. "Count on it."

I drove back to my house in Kill Devil Hills, and I really don't remember driving at all. I must have been totally lost in thought. I knew what I wanted to do, but I also knew I needed to think it out carefully before I acted.

What I wanted to do was to call on Bugs Away, check them out. See if there was anything about them—maybe one of the workers, or someone there—that helped confirm or dispel anything other than the coincidence that put the company servicing the houses of all three women shortly before their rape and murder and attempted rape. Of course, it was not that unusual to be using the same pest control company, especially if the owner himself was eager enough to be soliciting business.

I guess the only question I had now was whether to wait for Balls to, as he said, "check them out."

After all, I thought again, I *was* a homeowner, with a house not far from the water, and the other night I had seen a water bug—or cockroach—scurry under one of the kitchen counters when I flicked on the light.

Made perfect sense for me to stop by the business and make a few inquiries about prices and so forth.

Chapter Twenty-Four

I decided to wait until the next morning to call on Bugs Away. This would give Balls time to "check things out," in case he got around to it. But there was absolutely no reason that as a homeowner I could not get on the schedule to have my little house debugged.

The night before, I had gone over to Elly's for dinner—or supper, as we most often called it. As always, the meal was delicious. Mrs. Pedersen served shrimp, sautéed with a splash of olive oil, white pepper, a sprinkle of marjoram, and a vague dusting of Old Bay Seasoning; corn off-the-cob; coleslaw that she had made from scratch; green peas that Martin liked very much—even more than the shrimp—and those biscuits of hers which were excellent as a sort of dessert with honey-butter in a scalloped-shaped dish we passed back and forth. Of course, there was cocktail sauce for those who wanted it, made with fresh horseradish, catsup, and a pinch of sugar.

After the meal, Elly and I sat on the front porch swing and watched the night come on. A light breeze carried the scent of spring. Things were really beginning to grow. I loved the smell. And I loved the scent of Elly, sitting very close beside me. Shortly before we had come out, Martin showed me a sketch he had done of the swing and a portion of the porch. It was very good.

"He's got a lot of talent," I said to Elly.

"Yes, he does," she said. She took my hand. With a smile she said, "Did you notice that he drew a dog sleeping in front of the swing?"

"That was a nice touch," I said.

"A not-so-subtle touch," she said.

"He wants a dog?"

"All he's been talking about lately."

"Uh-oh."

"Yes, the campaign has begun."

"I'll bet I know how it ends."

"Well, we'll see . . ." she said.

Before leaving, I told Elly—as casually as I could—that I planned to speak to a pest control company the next day about getting my house treated.

She knew that I had a tendency to let such errands or projects consume my days, if I wasn't careful.

"What about the book? Any progress?"

"I hope I'll be able to spend a lot of time on it this summer," I said. Except for some short stories, most of my writing, especially in these past few years, had been true crime. But for a decade or more I had toyed with a novel I really wanted to write—centering on a jazz musician who tried to hang on to the music and the magic just when the big bands were going out of style. There had always been an element of sadness in that of entertainers who wanted to keep on keeping on, even after the pendulum of time and style had swung the other way. I had close to a hundred pages done. I vowed to get back to it—and leave off writing about murder and mayhem for a period.

But here I was the next morning preparing to drive up to Point Harbor on the pretense of having my house debugged.

I waited until after nine to leave. Balls had not called, and whether he'd gotten around to checking out Bugs Away was doubtful. I didn't call him or Odell. I'd talk with them later. After I'd made my visit.

Traffic had picked up moderately when I started out. It was the heaviest coming south, and I was heading north, toward the Wright Memorial Bridge at the end of the Bypass, or Highway 158. The bridge, almost three miles long, crossed over the Currituck Sound and ended at the line into Currituck County. The Currituck Sound is about thirty-seven miles long and stretches all the way to the Virginia line.

I always enjoyed going across the bridge. The view of the water, the sky and clouds varied from hour to hour. The color of the water changed too. Some days it was metallic gray. A few hours later it may take on a bluish tint . . . or brown. The water may be as smooth as glass. If the wind kicks up, there can be whitecaps and two-foot waves, and even more.

Although Highway 158 is designated as north-south, going across the bridge toward Currituck County, you travel due west. The Wright Memorial Bridge is really two separate bridges; each has two lanes.

Off to my left a couple of hundred yards or more, there's a structure that looks like a duck blind. One of the long-time residents of Currituck said the structure—maybe it *is* a duck blind—actually marks where four of the sounds converge— the Currituck, Roanoke, Croatan, and the Albemarle, along with the end of North River, which runs along the west side of the peninsula that comprises the lower portion of Currituck County.

The sounds and the ends of the rivers make up what is known as the Greater Albemarle Sound. To the south is the even larger Pamlico Sound. I've never been sure what the difference is between a sound and a bay. But I think a sound is more enclosed, with brackish water; and a bay opens to the ocean or sea and the water is saltier. Or, heck, maybe they're used interchangeably, which is often the case I suspect.

That spring day was beautiful. The water in the sound was not as dark as it is some days, the sky was a bright blue, and the wind was light and variable. I didn't drive much over fifty-five because I was enjoying looking around. Two vehicles—one a Virginia car, one a work panel truck of some kind—passed me going much faster.

At the end of the bridge, I was in the area known as

Point Harbor. There are no incorporated townships in Currituck County.

The Bugs Away business was a couple of miles away, on the west side of the highway. I saw the little building. It looked like a combination log cabin and a more traditional structure, with conventional vinyl siding of light tan along a good half of the outside. A large shed of the same kind of vinyl siding was attached to the rear of the building. I assumed that was where the insecticides and other equipment were kept. Two vehicles occupied the parking area on the left side. In front facing the highway, a tall sign on two columns, had dark red letters on a white background that read "Bugs Away," and then below that: "Professional Exterminators." Anther line, in black letters proclaimed, "We keep the Bugs Away." I pulled in beside one of the vehicles.

Inside, there was a small reception area, with a fortyish woman behind a small desk. Two rather plain visitors' chairs were side-by-side along one wall. There was no chair in front of her desk. The woman looked up at me as if she were surprised to see anyone. She wore glasses that made her eyes look large. She had on a red top with white letters over her left breast that said, "Bugs Away." The colors were reverse of those on the sign out front.

Her desk was bare except for a telephone with three or four buttons on the base, a small notepad/calendar combination, and one pen. The walls were as Spartan. Two pictures, one on the left wall and one on the wall to the right of the woman's desk, hung perfectly straight. One was a beach scene with sand dunes and sea oats; the other was a rendition of the space shot of the Outer Banks, showing the entire one-hundred-mile length of the thin barrier islands.

She clasped her hands in front of her on the desk, but barely on the desk because she had drawn her hands close to her body. "Yes?" she said. She made the word sound very tentative.

Beaming what I hoped was my most disarming smile, I

said, "Hi, I'm Harrison Weaver. And you are . . . ?"

"Eunice?" she said. A question rather than a statement.

"Eunice, I want to inquire about getting my house treated. Make the bugs go away." I smiled brightly again.

"Oh, yes," she said. "Let me get Mr. Javiner." She glanced over her right shoulder toward the door behind her. The door was almost closed, but didn't appear clicked shut. Judging by the size of the building, I figured there couldn't be more than one or two rooms behind the reception, plus a restroom, and maybe a closet.

The door behind Eunice opened and a tall Mr. Javiner appeared, extending his hand and smiling broadly. He looked no more than forty, maybe even a couple of years younger than Eunice. His hair was sandy, smartly trimmed. His eyes were browner than his hair. He wore neatly slim chinos and a pale green button-down oxford-weave dress shirt. Like many of us here at the Outer Banks, I think he'd done much of his shopping for clothes at Lands' End or L.L. Bean.

He introduced himself as Haskin Javiner, with the accent on the first syllable of his surname. I told him my name and we shook hands.

"Come into my office," he said warmly.

His office was only marginally less Spartan than Eunice's reception area. He moved around behind his desk and, before taking his seat, motioned with one hand for me to take the seat in front of his desk. The chair was small, almost of the style generally considered a secretarial chair.

He had a larger calendar/appointment book open in front of him; a telephone with two buttons; a seashell-shaped clear glass paperweight, with no papers under it to be weighted down. Lined up on the left side of his desk were at least a dozen pens and pencils. They were arranged neatly by color and by size.

Even seated I could scan the open appointment book and read Javiner's notations. As a reporter, I guess you learn to read upside down. A good ability to have, if you're nosey, which I am. I remember that my father, who worked as an editor at daily newspapers back in the day when a few papers were still using hot-type, would go back in the composition room of the paper and stand before a large table where the production head arranged lead type in a frame. He could do a bit of editing at the table—because he had learned to read not only upside down but backward too. Quite a feat.

No pictures adorned Javiner's walls, only a large monthly calendar from Print Plus in Kitty Hawk. A door to the side of his desk led, I presumed to a hallway, probably a restroom, and another door beyond to the shed. A good-size window with a slatted blind dominated the wall that looked out to the parking area to the left of the desk. Behind Javiner's chair, a two-drawer file cabinet occupied a space alongside a black floor-model safe. The safe was about two-and-a-half feet square, with a combination knob in the center of its door. A leather notebook on top of the safe partially obscured small gold script letters spelling out the manufacturer of the safe.

"So, Mr. Weaver, you'd like to make those bugs go away?" That warm smile most evident.

"Yes, I would. I think maybe one treatment would hopefully do it. I don't have many."

"Well, as you know, they don't come out so you can count them. The little rascals can hide quite effectively. We can, of course, do one treatment, but I would suggest you a monthly plan, with a considerably reduced rate than the one-time treatment."

We talked a bit more about price and scheduling and all the while I was trying to figure out a way to bring the subject around to treatment by Bugs Away at the two murder women's houses and at Lila's.

Out of my peripheral vision I saw the white panel Bugs Away truck pull past the window to park near the shed.

Javiner saw the truck also. "Oh, here's my chief go-to person for treatment, returning triumphantly from making another person's home free of insects." He stood and opened the door on the back wall. "I want you to meet him."

A big guy lumbered into Javiner's office. He was an inch or two taller than Javiner's six feet. He wore a red short-sleeved shirt with white letters like Eunice's with the company's "Bugs Away" words. His arms, hanging down by his side, were long and his hands huge. He didn't smile.

"This is Greg Ryan," Javiner said. "He trained with Bo at one of our competitor's. I was able to lure him away with promises of riches."

Javiner introduced me. I extended my hand, but Ryan didn't move, so I let my hand drop.

Ryan did mumble, "I know who he is." He nodded his head almost imperceptibly.

"Mr. Weaver is interested in at least an initial treatment at his house in Kill Devil Hills," Javiner said.

"The Kreigline folks canceled. I could do him tomorrow," Ryan said.

"You're in luck," Javiner said. "What time?" He glanced at the open appointment book on his desk. I wasn't sure whether the question was directed at me or at Ryan.

"I can do him the second thing," Ryan said. "Ten. That's when the Kreiglines were scheduled."

"Ten would be perfect for me," I said.

Javiner made a notation of my address and phone number in his appointment book, and the same information on a slip of paper he extracted from the middle drawer of his desk. He handed the paper to Ryan.

Ryan said, "Let me tell Eunice." He moved toward the reception area.

"I heard," Eunice called out.

Ryan continued anyway. As he passed by where I was seated, I couldn't be sure if he hadn't glared down at me. Still no smile. Maybe that was his normal countenance. That "taking no shit" look.

I heard a murmur of voices from Eunice and Ryan but

not loud enough for me to understand what they were saying. "He's the best," Javiner said. "You'll be pleased. And I do hope you will consider our monthly plan."

"I certainly will," I said, and I rose. So did Javiner, and he extended his hand. We shook hands and I told him I looked forward to seeing Ryan tomorrow morning at ten.

In the reception area, Ryan and Eunice stopped their conversation as I entered. "Glad to have met both of you," I said.

Eunice said, "Yes?"

To Ryan, I said, "See you at ten." Standing next to him, I could see how tight the short sleeves were because of his biceps. He was easily six-two or maybe even six-three. Two hundred pounds. He was certainly not the type of guy I'd want coming after me, and I can hold my own under most circumstances.

He nodded. "Ten." He still didn't smile.

As I drove back toward the Wright Memorial Bridge and Kitty Hawk, the first thing I'd do when I got home would be to call Balls, maybe Odell, too.

In addition to checking out the Bugs Away business, I wanted him to do a quick check on Greg Ryan.

I wanted that done before ten tomorrow morning when Ryan would be at my house.

Chapter Twenty-Five

Balls answered his cell on the second ring. "Whadda you want?" he growled.

"Where are you?"

"What damn difference does it make?"

"Didn't want to disturb you if . . ."

"When'd that make any difference to you?"

I shook my head and grinned. Good ol' Balls. I really liked him. "Wondering if you've had a chance to check Bugs Away, like you said you would."

"What's it take a village to keep you going? Yeah, believe it does." Then he got more serious. "Matter of fact I did. Didn't find out much, though. They've been in business here at the Outer Banks for less than a year." He paused, maybe to check his notes. "Run by a guy name a Javiner. Haskin Javiner." Another brief pause. "He's from your old neck a the woods. Northern Virginia. His business was in Leesburg."

"I know the area," I said.

"Trouble is, I don't know why he left. Or much else about him."

Then I told Balls that I'd met Javiner.

"I told you to stay away," he said.

"As a homeowner, I figured . . ."

"Okay, okay."

"His chief worker—guy named Greg Ryan—is coming here to my house tomorrow to treat for insects. Fact is, I'd like to know something about him. He's local, I'm pretty sure."

"Odell'd be the one to check on him. Or someone working with Odell," Balls said. "I got other things a do beside trying a keep you outta trouble."

"Appreciate it, Balls. You're a great humanitarian."

"Yeah, screw you, too."

Then, just like that, the banter was over. "You think there's a connection with this outfit—Javiner or this Ryan fellow—that in some way may lead us somewhere?" he said.

"Have no idea. Interesting, though, that a relatively new business had contact with all three victims . . ."

"Yeah, but I'm sure they had other business going on at the same time," he said.

Before we disconnected, Balls made known his frustration that they were making no progress at all on the investigation. As if he had to tell me that; I knew there was no progress.

Sitting there no more than a few minutes after the exchange with Balls, I took a deep breath and placed a call to Odell. I got his voice mail and I left him a message that I was trying to find out something about Greg Ryan, and why.

Late that afternoon, while I was actually doing some preliminary editing on my novel and really looking forward to spending time with it this summer, I got a call back from Odell.

"Found out some stuff about Greg Ryan," he said. "That worker for Bugs Away, and probably the one who did Ms. Quenton's house. The way she described the worker that came to her house."

"Yes," I said.

"He's had a couple of run-ins," Odell said. "Makes him interesting. Nothing major. Arrested twice on assault charges. One for a barroom fight with a couple of beer-drinking buddies. And once for something more interesting—assault and battery charge brought by an ex-girlfriend. Nothing much came of any of the charges."

"Thanks, Odell," I said.

After a brief pause, he said, "My opinion, he seems like a lot of guys around here. Sort of rough and quick temper that can get him in trouble. But no worse or no better'n a lot of them. But this does make him interesting. Someone we gotta talk to." Another short hesitation. "I'm sure Agent Twiddy's gonna want to talk to him."

Now it was my turn to pause, to hesitate before I said anything else. Then I said, "Actually, Ryan is coming to my house in the morning to treat for bugs."

Odell took a few seconds to process that. "Have you told Twiddy?"

"Yes, I mentioned it to him earlier today . . . briefly. He suggested I ask you about checking on his background."

It was obvious neither of us knew how to proceed. We sort of hung there on the phone a bit longer.

Finally, I said, "I won't try anything. You know, step into the investigation. I'll just be observant."

"And careful," Odell said. "Be careful." Then he tried to get some humor back into the conversation with a fake accent. "You know how you honkies can be. Get your heads all tore up without even trying."

I chuckled. "Ain't hit da truth," I said, adopting an exaggerated Southern vernacular.

Later on, I called Elly at work. A short conversation, but long enough to tell her I'd spent some time that afternoon on the novel. She was pleased. And I told her I would call that night, as usual.

I went to bed before ten and was up early the next morning. Greeted the sunshine and warm spring morning on the front deck with coffee. Maybe it was real, maybe not, but I always sensed I could actually smell the clean salt air coming off the ocean on days like this.

I busied myself with mindless chores that morning, keeping an eye on the clock. I fed Janey and made a mental note to caution Ryan about insecticides and my parakeet.

Shortly before ten, I went back out on the front deck,

which looked out over the cul-de-sac. Within five minutes, the Bugs Away white panel truck pulled slowly on to my street. He reversed the truck and pulled it in as far as he could to the rear side of my Outback. There would be almost no room to maneuver out, if I needed to.

The driver's side door opened, and Greg Ryan unfolded himself and stood tall beside the truck. He looked up and saw me. I raised a hand in greeting. I think he nodded a reply.

This was going to be an interesting day.

Chapter Twenty-Six

Ryan lumbered up the outside stairway, a plastic, handled carrier in one hand and a pump spray in the other. Muscles and veins stood out on his arms. Yes, he'd be a good one to have on your side in a barroom fight.

"How you doing, Ryan?"

"Okay," he mumbled. He glanced at Janey. She chirped happily because of the activity. "I'll be careful of the bird," he said. It was the most he had said since meeting him, and it was the most humane. "I'll only be spraying around the base-board."

I said, "It's warm enough. I'll put her outside on the deck."

He nodded. "Bird'll be all right. I'll make sure. But won't hurt to put it outside." He set the carrier on the floor near my desk/dinette table. He pumped the spray a couple of times and set to work. He started near the sliding glass doors. When he finished there, I pushed one of the doors back and carried Janey outside. She bobbed her head in appreciation as she greeted the bright sunshine.

I watched him work and tried to imagine a rape/murder scene. I had difficulty conjuring that up. And I had an even more difficult time getting a mental picture of Lila Quenton kicking him in the groin and making a successful escape. Maybe that was a good thing—that I had trouble envisioning a rape and murder.

When Ryan got around to the side of my living room near the bass fiddle, he stopped, looked at me and smiled. Actually smiled. First time I'd seen anything other than a scowl. "I've heard you play that thing," he said. "You're good."

"Thanks," I said. Obviously, he'd been at one of the clubs where Jim Watson's jazz combo had played, or maybe at one of the afternoon gigs at Scarborough Faire. But a beer-drinking club made more sense.

Before he went into the two bedrooms to finish up spraying, Ryan stopped and turned toward me. "After you left yesterday, Mr. Javiner wanted to know how I knew you . . . and all about you. He didn't know you wrote about murder and everything." He stopped.

"Yes?" I said.

"He wanted to know if you were some kind of investigator or detective or something."

"I'm just a writer," I said.

"That's what I told him. But I said you did get sort of mixed up in the middle of things."

"That's not my job."

He nodded and went back to spraying the second bedroom I use more for storage than anything else.

Why was he telling me this? Did he suspect I was in the middle of this one? Was it really Ryan, and not Javiner, who was most interested? But maybe Javiner did really press Ryan regarding how much he knew about me. And it was surprising that Ryan seemed to know so much about me—that I played with a jazz combo, and that I had a tendency to get mixed up in the middle of investigations.

Be careful, be careful.

Ryan finished the one bedroom and moved into my bedroom. He leaned over the bed to spray along the baseboard, and then he slid my bedside table a few inches to get back there. I thought about my old .32 revolver, which Balls refers to as a peashooter, that is stored wrapped up in an old sock in the top drawer of the bedside table. I'd given thought earlier to possibly secreting it in the back waistband of my slacks and have it there before Ryan arrived. I'd discarded that thought rather quickly, admonishing myself for momentarily giving into what was surely a bit of paranoia. But on second thought, maybe not such a bad idea.

When he finished the bathroom and little hall, he stopped to give a couple of pumps to his sprayer. "I'll do the kitchen and inside the cabinets and then go outside to go around the perimeter of the house, and be through," he said. Then he added, "Oh, haven't put the chair and table back in place in the bedroom."

"Don't worry. I'll get that." Actually, I wanted to use the excuse to retrieve my peashooter and stick it in my back waistband, hide it under my pullover shirt.

It was time to get aggressive with my conversation with Mr. Greg Ryan.

He was standing more or less upright when I returned to the kitchen area. He had set the sprayer on the floor near his feet and placed both hands into the small of his back, pressing as if to get out the ache. I positioned myself at the end of the counter, where Janey's cage normally rested. Except for the upper part of my body, the counter hid me.

"Speaking of getting mixed up in the middle of things, you've done that yourself," I said.

His face screwed up, questioning. "Huh?"

I shrugged, with what I hoped was a disarming gesture. Plunging straight ahead, and maybe foolishly, I said, "Bugs Away did Francine Ferguson's house and also Trigger Massey's. Not long before they were raped and murdered."

Now that scowl came back full force. He glared at me. I held his searing gaze. I tried to give something of a smile. I didn't want to rile him too much. He moved closer to the counter.

Almost imperceptibly, I eased back from leaning on the counter. With what I hoped was a casual movement, I put both hands on my hips, one hand not far from the handle of the .32 caliber revolver.

"What do you mean, Mr. Weaver?" He moved even

closer to the counter. The full force of that glare aimed right at me. His huge lower jaw jutted out. "What the hell do you mean?" He was one mean looking son of a bitch.

I attempted another shrug, but my right fingers almost touched the grip of my gun. "I'm not implying anything—other than this is a small sandbar and we all get mixed up in things."

He put one of his large paws on the edge of the counter. His fingers were curled and his knuckles white. "Start with, I didn't do the Ferguson woman's house. That was afore I came with Bugs Away. Still in training with Bo over at the other place. Javiner did that one, along with this kid who worked about a week."

His face was only a few inches from mine. I could smell his breath and see the stubble on his face. My fingers touched the handle of my revolver. Ready.

"And another thing, and you better damn-well know it: Trigger was a friend of mine. I mean not a close friend or anything, but she was always so nice to me. I ate at most places where she worked. She called me by name and was always real nice to me, even when I was in that . . . that trouble."

I eased back a bit. "Ryan, I didn't mean that . . . I didn't mean to imply there was some sort of connection, just that we *do* get mixed up in things that . . ."

He relaxed somewhat. He stood straighter and drew back his face.

"Trigger was a nice person," he said again. His countenance lost some of its fierceness.

I removed my fingers from the revolver's handle.

He seemed to be playing a thought over in his mind. Standing there, he cast his eyes downward, the thousand-yard stare.

Okay, time to bring on something else. Catch his reaction.

"At least that Quenton woman wasn't raped and murdered. Managed to get away."

Startled, he looked up at me. "Huh?" His head tilted to one side. "What Quenton woman? Whadda you talking about?"

"Down in Nags Head. Lila Quenton. Bugs Away did her house about a week ago and then the other night, some guy tried to rape her—maybe murder her too—but she managed to escape."

Puzzlement wrinkled his brow. "You mean the woman what works for some real estate outfit. Has the little brown house near the sound?" He shook his head. "Something happen to her?" His face screwed up with concern, or distress, it might have been. "Yeah, I did her house. First thing in the morning. She'd made 'rangements to go into work later that morning."

I said, "Figured maybe you'd heard about it by now. Not exactly a secret. But she managed to get away."

"I sure as shit didn't have nothing to do with that one either," he said.

And I had to believe him. He wasn't faking that surprise. I've done enough interviews over the years to have a pretty keen sense of when someone is bullshitting. He wasn't.

Ryan laid both hands on the counter. It was not a threatening move. It was more like he needed the support. He gave another shake of his head. "Can't believe something happened to her. Hell, I was just there." He bored his sight into my face. His chin jutted out, and he repeated, "And I sure as shit didn't do nothing to her, neither."

"Don't mean to imply that you did, Ryan. It's curious because all three of these houses owned by these women were serviced by Bugs Away."

Ryan said, "Yeah . . . yeah, I know." But I thought his mind centered on something other than his response. He concentrated, wrinkling his forehead; then one hand came up and he wiped it across his face. Erasing a thought?

Okay, he was in the mood to talk. Time to keep at it.

"But I am curious, Ryan. How does Bugs Away get its business? I mean it's a new company. Fairly new. Advertising? Word-of-mouth? You go around?"

"Yeah, all of that, I guess. 'Cept I don't go around. Mr. Javiner does. Makes calls, talks to people. He's a smooth talker." Ryan answered me but I still felt his mind was elsewhere.

"Tell me, Ryan, how is Mr. Javiner to work for? I don't mean to pry . . . well, yes, I do. One of my primary characteristics."

"Huh? Oh, he's not bad to work for. Peculiar, I guess. In some ways. Wants everything kept in strict order. Hell, you ought a see my workshed, where we keep the chemicals and all. Everything gotta be 'ranged in some sort a strict order."

We stood there silently for a full minute or more. Each of us apparently nursing other thoughts, I was convinced, but with a common thread—the rape and murder of two women and the attack on a third.

Ryan straightened his stance, flexed his shoulders as if to loosen them. That look of concern still on his face. He shook his head, took a full breath, and then glanced at his watch. "Let me get the outside."

But he paused and looked again at my face. "Woman down in Nags Head escaped. How'd she do it?"

"Kicked the guy in the balls and ran like hell."

Ryan almost grinned. "Good."

He started to take the sprayer, stopped, and picked up the container. "I'll come back up when I'm finished. Won't take but a few minutes," he said. He pointed his head toward the sprayer. "Get that then."

At the kitchen door, he said, "You can bring your bird back inside if you want."

Janey appeared to be enjoying the sunshine outside and the warm, almost windless, day. A windless day was a real rarity. I know she missed the activity in the kitchen when Ryan and I were talking. She would have wanted to join in, as she always does when I'm on the telephone.

No more than ten minutes later, I heard Ryan coming back up the outside stairs. I kept the gun, still in my waistband. Just in case. I felt rather foolish, maybe. But didn't hurt having it until he was gone.

"I need to settle up with you," I said when he came into the kitchen.

"You can pay me or just wait for a bill from the company or stop by or whatever suits you," he said.

I hadn't gotten enough from him yet. As he bent to pick up the sprayer, I said, "You said Mr. Javiner was peculiar. In what other ways?"

He stopped and looked over at me, the beginning trace of a grin on his face. "Well . . . You know I said Mr. Javiner was a smooth talker? Yeah, well he is. He can be a funny talker sometimes, too, when he wants to be."

"Yes? What do you mean?"

"I mean funny, like he can do something funny with his voice. I don't know whether he puts something in his mouth to sound that way or whether he can do it with his own voice. But he can sound real different. Like that bad guy in, you know, *Star Wars*."

My throat felt like cold fingers clutched it. But I managed to say, my voice weak, "You mean Darth Vader?"

"Yeah, like that guy." Holding the sprayer alongside his thigh, he turned toward me. "He did that one time for Eunice. Scared the shit outta her."

"I'll bet it did," I said, my voice still sounding off-key.

Then I managed to say, "I'll plan to stop by first thing in the morning. Pay then. He wants to talk with me anyway about signing on for a monthly deal."

Ryan left.

I leaned heavily on the counter. And now I was the one with the thousand-yard stare.

Chapter Twenty-Seven

After a while—I don't know how long I propped myself up by the counter—I went to the phone and placed a call to Balls. No answer. Left a brief message to call me. Then I tried Odell. Same thing. No answer. I was about to leave a voice mail when Mabel picked up.

"I saw it was you," she said. "They're both—Agent Twiddy and Odell—are all the way down at Buxton, if they've got there yet, and they'll be there all day. They've got two interviews, I know." She took a heavy breath. "Anything I can do for you, Mr. Weaver?"

"What's this *Mister* Weaver crap?"

She chuckled. "Okay. Anything I can do for you, honey?"

"It's not 'honey.' It's 'sweetie.'"

Now there was a full chuckle, and I could hear her breathing.

"No, Mabel, but I appreciate it." I was about to disconnect. "Oh, if you can transfer me to Elly, that'd be nice."

"Hold a second, sweetie. I'll switch you to your sweetie."

The light chatter did make me feel marginally better. I was determined to not let my voice betray me as I spoke with Elly. Janet answered and then handed the phone to Elly. "Wanted to give a quick hello," I said. "Exterminator finished up treating the house—and not Janey."

"Good," she said.

I could tell she monitored my voice to discern if there was something else there that needed to be said. She was good at that.

"I'm going to hang around here the rest of the day. Get

some work done," I said.

She paused a moment. "Stay out of trouble," she said.

"Oh, I will. You know me."

"Yes, I do. That's why I said that."

"See you tomorrow night?"

"That would be nice," she said.

After we hung up, I continued to sit there by the telephone a few minutes. I was a little at loose ends, as we say in the South. Then I had a thought about a follow-up call I'd wanted to make. I went to my desk, looked up the number in my list of contacts, and took the phone with me outside on the deck and took a seat next to the table on which Janey's cage rested. She did her head-bobbing little dance, happy to have company other than the pesky blue jay who ate seeds I put out on the railing.

I prepared to call my friend Michael Rohrer, a detective with the Loudoun County Sheriff's Office. Michael also happened to be the principal bassist with the Loudoun Symphony Orchestra. That's where I had first met him, when I had started playing with them, shortly after Keely died—had killed herself—and I didn't think I wanted to play jazz anymore.

Michael was an excellent classical bassist who could also play jazz. A rare quality. For classical, it's mostly arco, or bowing, and very little pizzicato, or plucking, as there is in jazz.

There were four of us playing bass regularly with the symphony. Interesting to me was that two of us—Michael and me—used the French bow, and the other two used the German bow.

The French bow is held with the fingertips, somewhat delicately, much as a violin player holds his or her bow. The German bow is held like a pistol grip. I know it's stereotyping, and you shouldn't do it, but I couldn't help but toy with the idea that the different bows represented the difference in the basic characteristics of the two groups of people —the French and the German.

Michael was also a very good detective.

I dialed the number I had for him. To my utter surprise, he answered on the second ring. I thought I would have had to go through the punch-this or punch-that button, and then leave my number hoping he would call back.

It was good to hear his voice. In no time at all we had caught up with what had been happening with our music. It was like we were comfortably chatting, following the usual Wednesday night rehearsal. He did tell me that in the next concert the symphony was going to do Beethoven's Ninth. Michael said it would probably take him the six weeks before the concert to get the bass part down right. It is a real toughie, but I knew, also, Michael would have the bass part nailed. A person in the audience could work up a sweat watching Michael's left hand maneuvering over the strings.

Then we turned to criminal investigations, and I briefed him on what was going on here with the rapes and murders. I said I was curious if there had been any similar cases in his area.

He didn't hesitate. "Not in little more than a year," he said. "But we do have two still unsolved here in the county, one in Leesburg and one in Purcellville. Before that—actually in between the two here—there was a similar one over in Orange."

"Same M.O. in all three?" A chill began to develop down my spine.

"Yes."

"Anything stand out in your mind about them?" I said.

"You mean beyond the fact that the bastard is still out there somewhere, unless he's dead? And the fact that there was no forensic evidence at all? Victims manually strangled. Condom used."

More of a chill.

"Anything else that stood out? Anything, well, sort of different about the scene or scenes?" I asked.

Now he did hesitate. He knew I wasn't simply fishing;

that I had something else in mind. Then he said, "You mean about no forensics?" Another hesitation, as if he didn't want to lead me. "Well, the scenes were . . . were extraordinarily neat. I mean not like most crime scenes."

The chill down my spine was now full-blown.

This time it was I who hesitated. "Clothes? Clothes neatly folded?"

He breathed out an expletive. "Yeah, yeah. Jeez, you got him down there?"

I thought about asking him about exterminators, but that might be premature. "No, we don't have him. But same M.O. down here. Clothes folded in a chair. Manual strangulation."

I knew another question was coming.

"All of the victims' clothes in the chair?" he said.

"Yes . . . almost all of them."

"No underwear? No panties?"

"Souvenirs. Got to be the same guy," I said.

"You got to get that bastard," Michael said.

"We will. I think we've got a solid lead on him . . . well, maybe."

Where the hell did I get that "we" bit? I had something of a lead, and it wasn't my investigation, but there was no way I could let it go. No way I could not move ahead with it. I couldn't help myself. It was like I was a dog on a trail, barking and sniffing, barking and sniffing.

Rohrer said, "Don't let him slip away. Bust him good. I'm sure we can pin these cases up here on him too."

"I'll . . . we'll . . . do our best," I said. "And I'll be back at you."

"Counting on you, Weaver," he said.

As we prepared to hang up, I said, "Work on the Ninth."

"Huh?"

"Beethoven's Ninth. Work on it. Good luck on it."

"Yes, it'll take luck . . . and a lot of perseverance,"

And I thought the same thing about what I was determined to face.

Chapter Twenty-Eight

The next morning, I prepared to go up to the Point Harbor portion of lower Currituck County to Bugs Away. I kept checking my wristwatch, and other timepieces in the house. I sat outside for a few minutes with a cup of coffee and one of my Honduran cigars. I put the cigar down, went back inside, and started to bring Janey out. Decided against it and went back outside.

Then I tried to force myself to relax, take it easy, enjoy the early morning sun and blue sky.

Neither Balls nor Odell had called. For all I knew, they were still down at Buxton. Maybe spent the night there. I was convinced they'd call at some point.

I checked my wristwatch again. I've now got one of those fancy watches that tells heart rate, blood pressure, everything else—and even the time of day. I knew my heart rate was up. Didn't need a watch to tell me that. This time I actually looked at the time, not just what time it wasn't.

Another ten minutes or so and I'd leave. Head for Bugs Away, and a visit to Mr. Haskin Javiner.

Inside, I checked on Janey once again. Spoke to her and put a sprig of millet seeds in her cage as a treat, which she appreciated with a couple of loud chirps and head bobbing.

I went into the bedroom and opened the drawer in my bedside table. The .32 revolver snuggled there in a big old sock, where I'd returned it after Ryan left. The revolver looked comforting. The gun was lightly oiled and some of the oil had rubbed off on the sock. The gun slid out of the sock quite easily and rested in my hand. Heavy, solid feeling.

I used the end of the sock to make sure any excess oil didn't get on my slacks, as I lifted my shirttail and pushed the gun into my waistband.

Standing straight, I turned slightly to the side and checked myself in the mirror on my dresser. Only a little bulge visible.

This is stupid, Harrison. You're not going to a shootout. Put the damn gun away . . . or at least take it out of your pants. Take it in the car if you want to, but you sure as shit don't need to walk into a business office armed. Get real, man. This is an interview; see if you can get any sort of hint from him and his actions that would prompt you to sic Balls and Odell on him.

At first, I had not the slightest notion as to how I was going to do that. But maybe the Darth Vader voice thing would do it.

I put the gun back in the sock, carrying by the end of the sock so it hung down and swung by my side.

"Okay, Janey, I'll see you later."

"Shit," she said, clearly as anything.

"Watch your language, girl," I said.

She bobbed her head to show there were no hard feelings.

Before starting the engine on my Outback, I sat there and breathed evenly. I had put the sock-encased revolver under the front seat. I had my checkbook with me, and a pen. But I smiled to myself and put the pen in the glove compartment. I would use one of his—Haskin Javiner's.

Traffic was light going north toward Wright Memorial Bridge. As I passed by the end of Duck Woods Country Club golf course, there was a foursome on the green closest to the Bypass. The thirteenth hole, I think it is. Good day for it. They got a fairly early start to be on the back nine by nine o'clock. Checked the time on the dashboard. Nine-twenty, actually.

Crossing the bridge, I always check the water in the Currituck Sound. Today it was smooth and a dull metallic color. The texture reminded me of the old-fashioned dimpled tin ceilings one used to see.

I still didn't know exactly how I would proceed with talking to Javiner, but I knew that settling my bill would certainly be the opening.

Pulling into the parking lot on the left side of Bugs Away, there was only one other vehicle there. A Lexus SUV. Had to be Javiner's.

I went in the front door. Eunice was not there. Her desk bare, as it mostly was anyway. No sign of her. The door to Javiner's office was partly open and I could see most of the way in.

"Come in," he called out.

I looped to the side of Eunice's desk and entered Javiner's office.

He sat behind his desk, his arms atop the desk. He wore a long-sleeved button-down shirt, Oxford weave. His hair was brushed neatly to one side and parted precisely. He didn't rise from his chair. The smile was there, but something was lacking in it today.

He nodded toward the chair in front of his desk and worked on that smile again.

I took a seat. "Ryan did a good job yesterday."

"I figured he would," Javiner said, but his voice didn't register any real enthusiasm.

"I thought I'd stop in this morning and pay for the service."

"You didn't need to do that. We could have invoiced you."

"I had to come up this way anyway," I lied. I held my fold-up checkbook in one hand, and I laid it on his desk, opened it and made a show of patting my pockets as if looking for a pen. His pens and pencils remained lined up in perfect order.

I reached for one of his pens.

And I let my fingers make a mess of the pen and pencil arrangement. I didn't knock any to the floor, but I twisted them so it looked almost like a kid had dropped a handful on the desk. The childhood game of Pick-Up-Sticks.

"Sorry," I mumbled, but as if it were no big deal.

He tensed. A look of what had to be pain creased his forehead and eyebrows. I looked up at his eyes. Yes, they were a dark brown. Very dark.

"Eighty dollars?" I said.

"Huh? Oh, yes, eighty." Then, almost by rote, he said, "You should consider the monthly plan." He looked down at his jumble of pens and pencils.

"Let me see how effective this first treatment is, and then I'll decide."

"Fine, fine. That'll work."

I started to write the check, using one of his ballpoint pens. It didn't want to get started. I mumbled something; I laid the pen down and picked up another one. "Just make it out to Bugs Away?"

"Yes," he said absently. "Fine."

This pen worked and I entered the date, slowly. Taking more time than I needed.

His hands twitched. As I wrote out the check, one of his hands appeared to have a life of its own, and it moved toward the pens and pencils and expertly straightened them out, lined them up, and then repositioned two of the pens in proper order.

At the same time, from my left through the window, I saw the Bugs Away panel truck pull up, and Ryan got out. He went straight to the shed. I knew the door behind Javiner's desk accessed the shed, and vice versa.

I carefully tore the check out of the checkbook and held it in fingers of one hand. "Want me to put this on Eunice's desk?"

Some motion in the shed could be heard as Ryan made his way through there, and toward the office.

Javiner appeared—what? addled? not really with it?—
"Oh, you can leave it here." He gave an involuntary jerk as
he heard the door begin to open. "Eunice is off today."

Ryan stepped into the office. He stood tall and unsmil-
ing two feet from the end of Javiner's desk. "She isn't just
off." He leaned forward slightly toward Javiner. "She quit."

"What? Quit?" A shudder appeared to slither across
Javiner's body. Maybe it was in the way Ryan spoke, as if
there were more to it.

And there was.

Ryan rested one huge fist on the edge of Javiner's desk.
He glanced at me. "I did some thinking after we talked yesterday. And then Eunice and I talked." He turned his attention back to Javiner. "She called me last night. She got into
your safe. She knows what's in there."

Javiner rose quickly and turned to look at his safe. His
movements were jerky, like a marionette operated by a
palsied hand. "The safe's closed. Always. She doesn't know
the code." He stared at his safe, then back up at Ryan.
Javiner was tall, but not quite as tall as Ryan.

With a challenge in his voice, Ryan said, "She figured
out your code. You have it written—in code—in the little
book on top of the safe. Took her a long time, but she figured
it out." He displayed a lopsided grin of victory. "She's not
nearly as dumb as you thought she was." Then he leaned in
even closer. "She told me what's in there." The grin was
gone, replaced by a hard glare of hate or defiance. "You're
one sick son of a bitch, Javiner."

I realized that at some point during the exchange, I had
risen also, so that the three of us stood in a triangle.

This was getting bad. I wished now I'd secreted my revolver in my waistband. It wasn't doing me any good out
there under the front seat of my car.

Ryan cast a quick glance at me and then back at Javiner.
"In the safe, all those women's panties. Your goddamn souvenirs. I know Trigger's panties are in there too, you bastard.

She never hurt anyone."

Javiner's face changed with growing rage. He trembled, not of fear, but with all-consuming anger. He took on the countenance of a different person. It was as if the bone structure of his face had shifted, distorted. Scary. Damn right it was scary. I'd never seen such a change in anyone. Like his face melted and then reformed.

"And that disguise, too, a rubber face and hat," Ryan said.

For maybe a second, we all three seemed to freeze. We were like a still photograph. A sepia toned picture.

Then there was a movement from Javiner. His jaw jutted out, almost as if dislocated. He spoke. The voice that came out enveloped me with dread. I rested my hands on the edge of the desk as support.

The voice was like Lila had described, like a Darth Vader voice. It was not human. "What the hell do you think you can do with this? Huh, Ryan? What do you think you can do?"

Javiner's hand moved quickly to the top drawer of his desk. "You're not going to be able to do anything with it." Javiner's hand held a dark-colored pistol. Probably a Glock. Semi-automatic.

Ryan lurched toward Javiner. But Javiner fired. The sound was loud and banged around in that small office, and I saw the muzzle flare at the business end of his pistol. Ryan's forward movement stopped as if he'd smacked into a wall.

Ryan sank back. He didn't fall, not immediately. He stared at Javiner and then at his chest and at a growing flow of blood coming out of his Bugs Away shirt. Ryan's eyes began to glaze, and I could tell his legs were about to give way.

Javiner appeared ready to fire again, and I knew I'd be next. In that brief period—it had to be less than a second—I knew what I had to do. I don't know how I did it, but I propelled myself over the top of Javiner's desk and hit him square in the chest with my shoulders.

We tumbled over. He landed on his back with me on top of him. He tried to maneuver the gun around so it was pointed at my head, but I grabbed his wrist and, using all the strength I had and using my feet and legs against the legs of his desk for even more leverage, I slammed his hand against the sharp edge of his safe. I slammed his hand again. The gun discharged upward, not far from my face. I felt the muzzle flare and heat against my cheek, and the sound was so loud I didn't think I'd ever be able to hear again.

Again, I slammed his hand again against the safe's edge. I did it again. Maybe again, and again. Then the gun slipped out of his hand, which was now bloody and probably had several broken bones.

As the gun fell to the floor, I used the elbow of the now free hand, to smack him hard in the face. I hit his cheek and then his nose. I jabbed down hard with my elbow, again and again. With my other hand, I made sure his arm was secured. I jabbed my elbow into his throat, and back to his face again. I felt him go limp.

I scrambled to my feet, holding his still warm gun in my right hand. Javiner lay there in a semi-conscious state, but I kept the gun trained on him, and I knew I'd shoot the bastard if I had to.

I backed to the side of his desk, stepping over his legs, and I picked up the phone, punched in 911.

I gave the information to a dispatcher. I had to do it twice because my breathing was so fast and ragged.

Making my way around the desk, I wanted to check on Ryan. He lay sprawled on his back, his shirt now soaked with blood. I felt his neck. There was a pulse, but it was weak. Very weak.

Javiner tried to rouse himself, but collapsed again before he could prop himself up. I had beat the shit out of him. No question about that.

I switched the pistol—it was a Glock—to my left hand and dried my right palm of sweat against my shirt, and then switched hands again.

Never taking my eyes or aim off Javiner, I knelt beside Ryan and said, "Hang on a little longer, partner. We got help coming. The cavalry'll be here soon. Hold on. Stay with me."

I was afraid he was dying. His breathing was ragged and bloody spittle came to his lips. I pulled on the tail of my shirt and wiped his mouth.

Trying to judge time at a moment like this was impossible. But it was probably not long at all before I heard a siren and then saw through the window the Lower Currituck Rescue vehicle kick up gravel coming into the parking area. Right alongside the ambulance, a Currituck Sheriff's cruiser arrived; two deputies emerged quickly. Then another plain car I knew belonged to one of the county's detectives.

"Back here," I yelled to the medics who came in the front. I put the Glock aside. Didn't need to have that in my hand when they came in. I moved out of the way, and they went right to work on Ryan. Very serious and shaking their heads.

I was standing when the two deputies came in. They didn't have weapons drawn, but their hands were at the ready.

Javiner struggled again, trying to get up. He almost made it.

I was trying to explain to the deputies what had happened. Naturally, I was their primary suspect for the moment. But I was in luck. I knew the detective who came in. "Chris," I said. "I am really glad to see you."

The medical techs prepared to get Ryan onto a gurney and into the ambulance. I heard one of them say they'd better summon the medical helicopter for a trip with Ryan to Norfolk, quickly, or he'd never make it.

Chris and another lawman got Javiner to his feet. They started to cuff him, hesitated because he was so wobbly he didn't appear he'd cause any trouble; then they decided better safe than sorry, and they cuffed him and with another detective who had arrived, they escorted him out to the cruiser.

I took the moment to sink down in the chair in front of the desk. My ears still rang, and I was so tired, I wasn't sure I could stand without wobbling like a drunk.

Chris slid Javiner's chair out from behind the desk, and he and I sat there facing each other, and I outlined for him exactly what had happened. He said he knew that Agent Twiddy would be talking to me.

"Oh, yes," I said. "I know."

About twenty minutes later, when I got ready to go, I took one last look at Javiner's desk. The pens and pencils were scattered over hell's half acre. I smiled to myself. Served the neat-freak bastard right.

Chapter Twenty-Nine

Greg Ryan made it. For several days, his condition was touch-and-go. They kept him in intensive care, of course, and he wasn't transferred to a regular room at the hospital until the fifth day. On the sixth day I drove up to Norfolk and visited him. He was still very weak, but he did acknowledge my presence, and I filled him in on details of what happened after he was shot.

Before I left, I made sure to convey messages from Odell and Balls wishing him well and thanking him for his part in the whole thing. I touched his hand and I also thanked him. I told him that he and Eunice had really been the ones who had pushed the investigation off dead center, and the ones who had prompted the action from Haskin Javiner.

I didn't stay long because I could see that Ryan wanted to go back to sleep.

After the customary judicial hearings—and I had to testify of course—Javiner was denied bail and held in various detention centers. He had been transferred two or more times. I think now he was up near Raleigh, awaiting trial back in Dare County. He's charged with at least two of the rapes and murders. The DA is pushing for first degree murder; Javiner's defense attorney will likely go for manslaughter, and not premeditated murder, claiming Javiner did not go to the women's houses with intentions of killing them.

At any rate, I'm sure Javiner is going to be put away for quite a while.

Balls' first reaction, of course, which he tried to mask with gruffness, was to admonish me for going to Bugs Away when he had told me to stay away. But I could tell he was pleased with what I'd done, and, yes, kind of proud of his "little buddy."

Balls and Odell were among the first to confront Javiner when he was in custody. Balls saw me the next day, and he said, "Somebody really did a job on Javiner's face. Beat the hell outta him." He looked at me, cocked his head. "You do that?"

I shrugged. "Got sharp elbows," I said.

Of course my editor, Rose, wanted a story, a full-length one. She said, "A book maybe?"

I wanted to get back to my novel in the coming summer, and the days were flying toward that time of the year. Tourist season would be in full bloom within a week or so.

Elly and I were spending as much time together as we could. In fact, that night I had a real date with her, and we planned to go to the Black Pelican for dinner and then walk out on the beach at dusk. The weather was cooperating beautifully.

After we ate and I had a coffee, we held hands and crossed Beach Road to go out on the beach. We placed our shoes at the end of a walkway and walked barefooted to the water. The sand was easier to walk on close to the surf. The tide was out, the ocean relatively calm. The surf rolled in toward us across the brown sand and faded out with a relieved sigh.

I held Elly's left hand and ran my thumb over the ring on her third finger.

"What are you thinking, Harrison?" she said.

"About us."

She squeezed my hand. "Me too," she said.

We were silent, walking along the edge of the ocean, the edge of the world.

Elly stopped and I stopped with her. She said, "I was thinking about the first time we walked together on the beach. You said we were meant for each other and you said,

'Let's always plan to walk along the beach, and let's plan to meet here again, at six o'clock some golden evening, a thousand years from now.'" She looked up at me. "Let's don't wait that long, Harrison."

I grabbed her and held her very tight. "We won't wait that long, dear Elly," I said.

With both hands on her shoulders, I ended our tight embrace and held her slightly away so I could look into her eyes. "That ring—that ring—is an engagement ring. We both know that in our hearts. We've known it from the beginning."

She smiled. It was a smile of love; maybe it was even a smile of acceptance, of sadness and of longing and of happiness and of everything rolled into one. It was that kind of smile and I'll never forget it.

I knew I smiled, too. "Will you marry me, dear Elly?"

Tears came in her eyes. She pushed herself into my arms and I held her as tight as before. "You know I will," she breathed.

When we walked back to get our shoes, we were both giddy with happiness, and we'd already started talking plans.

"We could get a house in the Mother Vineyard section of Manteo," I said. "I know of one that will be going on the market in a few months. Not on the market yet, and hardly anyone knows it will be available. Not too big, but four bedrooms. One for you and me, one for Martin, one as my office—a real office—and one as a guest room . . . or for your mother."

We practically skipped along the sand.

"Mother will want to stay where she is . . . and she won't be far away. And Martin won't have to change schools."

Our grins could have lit up the sky. We stopped to get our shoes. Only then did we let go of clasped hands.

We stood and Elly looked out toward the ocean and the edge of the world. "Let's do this again, Harrison. Let's make that promise."

I smiled and put my arm around her shoulders, and I looked out toward the edge of the world also. "Yes," I said, "Let's plan now to do this again . . . We'll be together always, and we'll celebrate an anniversary right here. We'll come here together, holding hands at six o'clock some golden evening, here at the beach, a thousand years from now."

CPSIA information can be obtained
at www.ICGtesting.com
Printed in the USA
LVHW090409020721
691685LV00005B/562

9 781622 681679